Through the Lock

Carol Otis Hurst

Houghton Mifflin Company Boston 2001
Walter Lorraine Books

Walter Lorraine (wr) Books

Library of Congress Cataloging-in-Publication Data

Hurst, Carol Otis.
  Through the Lock / by Carol Otis Hurst.
        p. cm.
  Summary: Etta, a twelve-year-old orphan in nineteenth-
century Connecticut, meets a boy living in an abandoned
cabin on the New Haven and Northampton Canal and has
adventures with him while trying to be reunited with her
siblings.
  ISBN 0-618-03036-0
  [1. Orphans—Fiction. 2. New Haven and Northampton
Canal (Conn. and Mass.)—Fiction. 3. Canals—Fiction.
4. Connecticut—Fiction.] I. Title.

PZ7.H95678 Th 2000
[Fic]—dc21
                                            99-028510

QUM 10 9 8 7 6 5 4 3 2 1

For Kay, for caring,
and for Vail,
for all the laughter and support

TABLE OF CONTENTS

THROUGH THE LOCK

1

Arrival

"Nothing like making yourself to home."

"Good Lord!" I jumped up, knocking over the chair, my hammer raised in my hand. I'd been so busy pounding butternuts and stuffing the nut meats into my mouth that I hadn't heard anyone come in. A tall boy, maybe two years older than I, stood by the open door. His hat was pulled low and I couldn't see his face.

He slammed the door with one hand while he took off his cap with the other and barked out questions.

"Who are you? What are you doing here? How did you find this place? Are you alone? Who sent you? Did anybody see you?"

I lowered my hammer arm. "Etta Prentice. Getting warm. Ran into it. Yes. Nobody. No." If he was going to throw questions at me, I'd throw answers right back. Sometimes a little humor will ease tensions, I've found, but his expression showed me it wasn't working this time.

His angry brown eyes looked me up and down.

That didn't take long; there's not much to me. Pa used to say I was no bigger than a pint of cider half drunk up. For a minute neither of us moved. I tried to read his face. Was he going to kill me or just throw me out? He looked mad enough to do either. I sidled over to the cobblestone fireplace, anxious for the fire's comfort but keeping my eyes on my questioner.

I'd started the fire as soon as I'd come in. There was a pile of logs and tinder and I had been too cold to wait for whoever owned this place to show up to grant permission. Now he was here, apparently, although he looked too young to own anything. Neither of us spoke as he turned to some pegs on the wall and carefully hung up his coat, scarf, and cap. Then he moved up to the fire himself and stared at it for a minute before turning to face me again.

"How long have you been here?" His eyes roamed about the cabin, seeming to check over every nook and cranny.

"Dunno. A half hour or so."

"Touch anything?"

"Well, lessee. I touched the door latch and then the tinderbox. Then I touched the wood and then—"

"Hush!" He gave me a scornful glance, shook his head, and walked around the room, stopping to pick up the chair I'd overturned. He pushed it back up to the table. I watched him, for the first time getting a better look at the place. It didn't take long. The cabin wasn't much; more of a shack, really just one big room—but it was spotless. The many cracks between the boards had been filled with something that looked like mud, only whiter. Each daub was even and smooth. In fact, everything in this cabin seemed even and smooth. Up against the walls were wooden boxes and barrels all carefully lined up.

He needn't have worried. I hadn't touched his things. I'd been too hungry and too cold to care about anything but getting a fire started and putting something into my stomach. The hard-to-crack nuts had been in a burlap sack on the floor, the hammer on a nail next to them, and my search had ended there.

When he turned back to me his frown was fierce, but I'd seen worse. "Look," he said. "You can't stay here. You'll attract too much attention." He peered out of the window as if crowds of people might be approaching.

"Did I ask you if I could stay here?" Of course, I had been about to ask that very thing, but I surely wouldn't let him know that. "I needed a way to get warm and I was hungry. I found this place. Thanks for the nuts." I put the last handful in my mouth before I walked to the table and grabbed my shawl and my carpetbag.

We both headed toward the door, with him in the lead. I gave a quick look around my temporary shelter and that wonderful, blazing fire, pulled my shawl around me, and started out the door. I couldn't get past him, however. He stopped in the doorway and reached up to pull a string of fish from a hook on the outside wall. He must have just put them there. They sure weren't there when I'd come in or I'd have had a stomach full of fish right then instead of a stomach growling over a few nuts. He nearly tripped over me when he stepped back inside. He drew back quickly and I stood aside to let him in. Then, before I could step out of the door, he slammed it.

"Fish," he stated flatly.

I looked at him warily. I wasn't sure whether he was offering me some food or taunting me with it. Heaven knew what he was going to do next. I thought about hanging my shawl up and then thought the better of it. That'd be taking too much for granted.

Ignoring me, he took a knife and a small cutting board from a nail on the wall and set about cleaning the fish at the table. I had a thought that he ought to do that outside because of the mess, but I held my tongue. Good thing, because he knew what he was doing. There was no mess and in no time a fish was gutted, beheaded, and boned. He picked up another. I let my breath out slowly. I was pretty sure now that one of those fish was for me.

He kept his eyes to his work and I stood where I was near the door, trying not to attract his attention away from the food preparation.

He looked up for a brief moment, knife poised over the second fish. "Walter Clark," he said and then went back to filleting.

I looked around to see if he was referring to someone or something behind me. There was nothing there. "Is that your name?" I walked closer to him. He nodded.

"Pleased to make your acquaintance, Walter. Is this your place?" I figured to get as much information as I could while he was in the mood to give it.

"'Tis now."

"How'd you come by it?"

He shrugged. "It was here when I was looking."

"Why is it here?"

"Part of the canal."

"Lockhouse?"

He looked disgusted. "Do you see a lock?"

"No," I said, glancing out at the canal.

"Foreman's shack." He spoke with his head down, concentrating on the task at hand. "He live here too?" I looked around. There appeared to be only one bed, neatly made and set over against the largest wall.

"Nope."

"Where is he?"

"Gone farther north, where they're digging now."

"Does he know you're living here?"

"Nope."

"Does anyone know you're living here?"

"Nope."

"What would you do if they found out?"

He shrugged. "Move."

"How old are you?"

"Twelve." He was younger than I thought he was, only a year older than I.

"Do you have family?"

"Enough!" He looked at me fiercely. I guess I'd pushed it a bit too far. At least I'd gotten some information before the well ran dry.

He got to his feet. I stepped back, afraid he was going to change his mind about the fish and usher me out. Instead, he scooped the discarded fish parts into his hand and walked outside. He was back in a minute to wash his hands in a pail near the fire. He took the pail to the door and dumped it. Then he took a pan down from the wall. He put in a dollop of grease and placed it on a trivet in the fireplace. "Eh-yah."

"Eh-yah?" I said.

"Eh-yah, I have family." He let his breath out heavily.

"I can see that conversation doesn't come naturally to you. Do you by any chance know the Halls over in

Hamden?" I grinned but he did not.

Instead, his scowl deepened. "Halls? No! How would I know them?" he barked.

"Just joshing," I said. "They hated talking too. Your family—do they know you're here?" I knew I was on dangerous ground.

He glared at me. "Did they send you?"

"Course not. I told you. Nobody sent me. Are they looking for you?"

"Not likely." He took an apple and two potatoes from a box and began to pare them. He was skillful with that knife. Probably a good whittler—Bertha would like that. The apple peel fell in one piece to the table.

"My Pa used to read your fortune the way the apple peel fell like that," I offered.

Again there was no response.

I tried another tack. "Did you catch the fish in the canal?"

"Good grief!" he shouted. "Will you never stop?"

I stood silent a minute and then went over to hang up my shawl.

Walter sliced the apple and potato into the pan with the fish and put it back on the trivet. I wanted to snatch a piece of the apple right then, but I didn't dare. I probably should have offered to help. He really should have cooked the potatoes first, then the apples, and then the fish. But somehow I thought my suggestions might be unwelcome. Anyway, it didn't take long before everything was sizzling. I don't think anything ever smelled as good as that food frying. It seemed years since I'd tasted anything really good to eat.

"Why did you leave?" I asked this timidly, afraid of his anger. Ma always said I never knew when to let well enough alone.

He jumped as if I'd shouted the question. Guess he'd forgotten I was there. "Leave what?"

"Leave your family, of course."

"Time to go."

If that was a conversation we'd been having, it stopped after that, mostly because I was taught not to talk with my mouth full. Actually, the meal wasn't awfully good. The apples were overcooked and the potatoes could have done with a bit more cooking, but beggars can't be choosers. I'd have eaten everything raw—including the fish—if I'd had to.

I thought to linger after we'd eaten, maybe even talk a bit, but Walter was on his feet as soon as the last bit left his plate.

"Where did you learn to cook?" I asked.

"Picked it up on my own," he said proudly. I helped him with the cleanup, hoping I wasn't going to be the one to go out into the cold to fetch water.

He wiped his mouth with the back of his hand and said, "I live here alone. I like it that way."

"And you do it very well too," I said. Maybe if I flattered him enough, he'd let me stay the night.

He walked over to the fireplace wall and pulled a plug out of a pipe. To my surprise, water ran into the pail he held beneath it.

He almost smiled when he saw my mouth fall open. "Snowmelt in the winter, rain run in the summer," he said, putting the plug back into the pipe. Right clever this contraption was and I spent just a minute admiring it, wondering how it worked and wishing that the houses I'd worked in, where every day I'd had to drag the water from the well to the house, had had the same setup. He put the pail on the now empty trivet and in a few minutes we were washing dishes in hot water.

We washed up in silence. As each thing was dry, he carefully put it back in its rightful place. When I tried to place things on various hooks on the wall, he very carefully moved them to another place or lined them up to be perfectly straight. This seemed silly to me but I didn't say so. Neither of us spoke.

I used some of the warm water to wash my face and hands. It felt good to be clean, at least in the spots that showed.

Now that I was fed, I kept thinking any minute he'd tell me to get going. My mind was casting about for a reason for him to let me stay but I couldn't come up with one. You'd think a boy living alone would need someone to cook and clean for him but he obviously had these things covered. Evidently he didn't think his cooking could stand improvement.

Walter jerked his head toward the rear of the house when I asked him where the privy was and, though I hated to face the cold again, I went outside. The winter's dark had descended and it was bitterly cold. I ran to the privy, holding my shawl tightly around me.

I know it's not possible for a privy to smell good but this one didn't smell bad and it was clean. Not a cobweb or a piece of dirt could I see anywhere. I didn't linger. The cold bit quickly in unmentionable places and I hurried back inside.

He was standing in the middle of the room.

"Why did you come?" he asked.

"That's a long story," I said.

"Shorten it," he said.

Perhaps if I told him how it was for me, he'd let me stay the night. "I didn't mean to. I came over the Connecticut line at Somers, then west across the river. I was following the canal hoping to find some sort of shelter when I stumbled onto your cabin. I'd been walking for two days and had long since run out of food. I'd spent most of what little money I had to cross the river on the ferry. I didn't know whether I'd freeze to death or starve first." I glanced at him. He had turned to look out the window and I couldn't see the expression on his face.

After a long while he said, "Anybody looking for you?"

"I'm not going back!" I shouted. He stepped back, startled. I shouldn't have spoken so loudly, but the thought of being put in another foster home, made to work from dawn to dusk, was too much.

I took a deep breath and then said, "I'm in a different county now and a different state. I made sure of that. I don't think they care enough to come after me. Besides, you're running away too, aren't you?"

"Nope," he said.

"Then why are you so anxious to keep this place a secret?"

He said nothing—just kept staring out the window. I stared out there too. I dreaded leaving.

"Look," he said, "you can stay the night but that's it."

"Oh, thank you," I said. "I'll go on in the morning."

"Eh-yah," he said, setting a blanket roll on the floor. As I gratefully headed toward it, he shook his head. "Use the bed," he said. "That's for me." His voice was flat and I sure wasn't going to argue. I dove into the bed in the corner quick as a fly to the meat.

The bed was comfortable, with two warm quilts on top. One quilt was a log cabin pattern and the other was eight hands round. I pulled the hands quilt up close. Even in the dim light you could tell the stitches were small and perfect. I looked over to see Walter watching me from his bedroll.

"Ma made 'em," he said, as he blew out the light.

2

My Story

At first light I jumped out of bed, hoping to cook the breakfast for us both, but Walter was already up and cooking.

The meal wasn't bad. When we'd finished eating, I said, "Thanks for letting me stay, Walter, and for the food."

He nodded. "Where were you living?"

"Lots of places."

"Parents?"

"Dead." I should have stopped there but I went on.

"After Ma died we—my brother and sister and I— were managing." I paused for a breath. "But we had no money for the rent. We should have been able to stay together somewhere else, like at my mother's brothers, but they wouldn't take us.

"So they split us up. I lived in lots of places. We all did. Bertha, she was twelve when we got split up, two years older than me—she went to Stafford to work in the carpet mills. She says it's all right but I can't imagine anything much worse. They shut her up tight in that awful, noisy, dangerous mill from six to six each day but Sunday."

This brought no response from Walter, but he didn't tell me to stop. At least the story was prolonging my stay here, where it was warm.

"Emory—he was eight when we got separated—they put him on a farm over near Somers. They're using him like a slave and he's so little." Just thinking about Emory almost made me tear up. It took a minute before I could go on.

Still Walter's face showed no response. Ah, well. When you're on a talking jag, even an unappreciative audience will do. "I promised the others I'd get us all back together again and I'll do it someday."

I looked again at Walter. He said, "What happened after you split up?"

Oh, he wanted more! I went on with new enthusiasm, settling back in the chair I'd been sitting on the edge of. "I lived with quite a few folks in Hamden and Somers after that. The Holliwells took me first. I suppose it isn't their fault that things didn't work out. I cried most of the time and folks will only put up with that for so long. They wanted a worker, not a sobber."

I wasn't sure, but I thought Walter's mouth twitched a bit. He was looking straight at me now. I waited a second, but he kept to his quiet and I returned to my talk. "Anyway, as soon as they could,

passed me over to the Kents. The Kents passed me on
to the Halls."

"The talkless ones," Walter said. So he had been
listening!

"Yes! They were all right, I guess, except for that.
Then they sent me on to the Peases. I didn't even say
goodbye to the Halls when I left. Just walked to the
buggy with my head up. Pride may goeth before a fall
but it also goeth a long way toward keeping your
dignity."

Walter glanced at me. Was that a smile? I decided it
was.

"So I was at the Peases. And the Peases were awful!
Kept the house cold enough to freeze the feathers off
a goose and then they'd eat the goose, while I got
nothing but whatever I could make out of the left-
overs. And you can bet your bottom dollar I didn't
get those till they smelled so bad even the Peases
couldn't stand it. But I had to pray over it. Mr. Pease
would hold forth for hours about counting our many
blessings. I couldn't find enough blessings in that
house to *name* let alone count.

"Anyway, a few nights ago, I lay there in the bed
under the eaves under the only blanket they'd given
me, seeing my breath in the moonlight, and I'd
suddenly had enough. Enough Peases and Halls and
all the other places I could see coming at me. I said to
myself, 'No more!' And I got out of bed, put a few

things in the old carpetbag, grabbed my shawl, and left. Walked right out the front door and I never looked back. And here I am."

I let out a deep breath and waited for a response. "Where are you headed?" he finally asked.

"I dunno. Someplace better." Even as I said it I knew that I had no place to go. There were no other relatives that I knew of beside Ma's brothers and, of course, Bertha and Emory. I'd already checked to see if the farm where Emory was staying needed more help, and I'd inquired at the other farms near him. I'd had no luck anywhere. I really wanted more than shelter anyway. I wanted a place not too far from Bertha and Emory so that we could see each other some and, eventually, live together. It wouldn't be the same without Ma and Pa. I knew that, but we could be a real family under one roof again.

I glanced at Walter. I thought maybe that I might have primed the pump and he'd return the favor and tell me all about himself. Besides, it felt so good to be full and warm and have somebody to talk to that I sat there drinking in the warmth that I knew would be over soon.

It was a long time before Walter spoke. "Pa drinks." Ah, I thought, here it comes. Now I get to hear Walter's story. But it didn't come. Walter only wiped his face with the back of his hand and got up from the table. He threw me a large wool cape, a big blue scarf, and some mittens.

"Whose are these?" I asked.

"Got them for my Ma," he said.

He grabbed a coat and cap for himself from the peg near the door and started out, pulling his gloves out of his sleeves. I put on the cape, scarf, and mittens and took up my carpetbag, then followed him out into the cold.

"Which direction are you headed?" he asked.

"I don't know," I said, "being unfamiliar with these parts. Maybe north." It was more of a question than an answer. I looked back at the cabin. "Are there more cabins like this somewhere?"

He shook his head. "Not that I know of."

"Well, thanks for the hospitality and for your mother's things. I'll bring them back, soon as I get settled. Goodbye, Walter," I said as I squared my shoulders and headed on up the canal. When I turned back, he was standing with his hands at his sides. He seemed to be waiting for something. Maybe I hadn't thanked him enough.

"Thanks again," I said, pulling the cape close around me.

"This way," he said.

"What do you mean? What's this way?"

"Work," he said. "If you're going to stay here, you've got to work."

"I can stay here?" I couldn't believe what he

was saying.

"For now," he said. "Just till we find you some other place. Put your bag back inside, then come with me."

I did what he said before he could change his mind.

When I joined him outside, the wind was blowing a bit, which made an already bitterly cold day even colder. The ice on the trees was thick and hard and the thin layer of snow creaked under our feet as we walked. Two crows up in one of the big trees were hunched over with cold, their heads down into their shoulders. They didn't move as we passed underneath them. Walter's long strides made him hard to keep up with, but I managed. It must have been zero, at least. Walter started down onto the frozen canal, then glanced at me. He turned to the towpath and we walked south next to the canal.

"Uh, where are we headed?" I couldn't stand not knowing. His head was down. So was mine. I pulled the hood of the cape up over my head and I'd wrapped the scarf around it but still the cold found cracks.

"Supplies," he said.

"Isn't it quicker to go on the road?"

"Eh-yah."

"Then why are we on the towpath?"

"Safer."

"Safer? Bears? Wolves? Moose?" I looked at him

anxiously. I hadn't seen any wild animals on my way here but there were many about, I knew.

"People."

"People who would find out where you're living?"

"Eh-yah."

You know, I could get tired of one-word answers rather quickly, but that was the sum total of talk till we got to Granby Center.

We seemed to be the only customers in the general store. A small woman stood behind the counter. She stared at us as we walked in. Walter took off his cap. A skinny boy was sweeping the floor. He glanced up for a minute, smiled at Walter, who nodded, and then went back to his sweeping. The woman's nod was brief and so was Walter's.

Walter said, "Pack of salt, pound of sugar, and one of cornmeal." She nodded and went off behind some shelves.

The boy stopped his sweeping. "He-he-hel-hello, Wah-Wah-Walt!" His face contorted as he tried to get the words out.

"Morning, Jake," Walter said, not batting an eye. "How's Minerva?"

"Fu-fu-fu-," Jake's whole body was engaged in the effort to speak.

"Boy!" The woman's voice stabbed the air, cutting Jake short. She plunked three sacks on the counter. "Tend to your business and leave the customers alone!" Jake was back in the corner sweeping before she could finish her sentence.

She scowled after him for a moment before turning back to me. "Who are you?" It was less a question than a demand.

I started to speak but Walter cut in. "My cousin," he said. She looked at me closely but said nothing. Then she turned back to Walter.

"How's your mother?" she asked.

"Fine," he said. He took two sacks and handed me the other and we were out the door. He didn't pay for them. Apparently, the stuff was free. Walter was some shopper.

"Walter," she called out. "Wood." Did everybody in this town carry on one-word conversations?

"Tomorrow," Walter said, and we hurried off.

"My! How you two did go on and on!" I said. "Why, I could hardly get a word in edgewise."

Walter darted a look at me and walked on as fast as he could, head down into his coat. In seconds he was yards ahead. I really had to run to catch up. When I did, he said, "Less she knows about us, the better."

I liked the sound of that "us" but thought it better not to push it. "Is Jake her son?" I asked, changing the subject.

"No." Walter's face softened a bit. "Don't know where he came from. Turned up there a year or so ago. She doesn't let him talk much."

"Hasn't got the time, I'd guess."

Walter whirled on me. "Don't you make fun of Jake!" His eyes flashed.

I stepped back. Although he didn't raise a hand, it sounded as if he was about to.

"Sorry."

"Jake does the best he can." He headed off down the road. In a minute I caught up again.

"Is Minerva his sister?"

"Cat." Walter's head was down again.

"Does Mrs. Sanford know your folks?"

"Eh-yah," he grunted. "Most folks know Pa."

"Does she just give you the food?"

He looked at me with disgust. "I pay for it with wood."

He turned away from me and walked even faster. The cold bit at my face and I pulled the scarf up onto it and let my breath warm my cheeks as I scurried after him. The cape was so much better than my worn shawl, large and thick, but even so, the cold air took advantage of every space it could find.

For a while we walked in silence. Eventually, I realized that we were not heading back to the house. "Where are we going?"

Walter jumped at my voice. Forgot me again, no doubt. "Wiltons. Supplies," he said.

"Ah, of course! Silly me to think we could live on cornmeal and sugar."

We walked on, each with our own thoughts. Most of mine were about the cold and trying to match my strides with his.

After a while I looked around at where we were going. We were heading west out of Granby Center into the hills, approaching a small farmhouse on the right.

As we came near, a large dog came rushing toward us, barking fiercely. Mind you, it's not that I'm afraid of dogs, but I've been around a few that would just as soon shorten your life as look at you so I stepped just to the other side of Walter. He put his hand out toward the creature, palm down, and said quietly, "Hello, Wolf." Well, the name was apt. The dog looked to be at least half wolf. Immediately, Wolf stopped in midrun and his tail began to wag so hard he seemed in danger of coming apart. He licked Walter's hand with great excitement and dropped to the road. He rolled over as Walter knelt to scratch the dog's belly. "Hello, Wolf. Good dog. Good fella." He scratched behind the dog's ears. Then he and the dog stood up and we continued into the dooryard, the dog nuzzling Walter's hand as he followed.

I'd been so busy keeping my eye on the dog that I hadn't noticed anyone come out of the house, but there was a man standing in the dooryard by the time we got to it. He was wrapped up against the cold and stamping his feet to warm up. He nodded and smiled.

"Morning, Walter."

"Morning." Walter's nod was brief. "Need some salt pork."

"Eh-yah. Hello, young lady." The farmer turned to me, a pleasant smile on his face.

"My cousin, Etta." Walter spoke before I could.

"Pleased to know you, Etta. I'm Ed Wilton. You live around here?"

"How do you—" I got no further.

"Eh-yah," Walter said, stepping in front of me. He needn't have worried. I wasn't about to give away any secrets. "Salt pork?"

"Right you are, Walter. Right you are. Cold enough for ya?" Mr. Wilton didn't wait for an answer but turned and headed into his house. Walter made no move to follow and motioned me to stay where I was. With Wolf looking at me suspiciously every time Walter's hand came off the top of his head, I wasn't about to move.

In a few minutes Mr. Wilton was back with a sack. He handed it to Walter. "When are you making the wood run?"

"Maybe tomorrow," Walter said, taking the sack.

"Another cold one, Walter, and the wind's getting stronger. May be blowing up a storm. Where are you living now?"

Here was a man who got right to it. I looked at Walter. "Granville," he said. His head was down.

"Near your folks?"

Walter nodded.

"Must have been cold coming down the mountain from Granville. I'd think you'd want to be closer to the canal than that." Now here was my kind of folks—a person who liked to talk and showed some interest in others.

"Eh-yah." Walter was turning to go but the farmer's hand on his arm stopped him.

"It's a long walk from Granville to Granby just for salt pork. Doesn't Avery have any?" This man was certainly not backing off.

"Had to come down anyway for some errands." Walter's eyes were on the dog. "Much obliged!" The dog followed us to the road.

"Stay, Wolf!" Mr. Wilton called, and the dog stopped midstride and sat down, gazing sadly at Walter as we walked on.

Mr. Wilton was right. The wind had come up even stronger, and we didn't go back the most direct way. Instead we made a beeline for the canal. This time Walter led me directly onto the ice, since the towpath and the berm on the other side of the canal offered some protection from the wind. It also kept us out of sight. Even so, the trip seemed to last forever. There was no point in trying to talk; the cold drove away any thought from our heads. Every breath came with its load of ice; we walked with our heads drawn into our clothing. The sight of Walter's house through the trees when we finally got near was such a welcome one that I began to run up and over the towpath toward it. Walter threw his sack across his back and joined me in the race. With his long legs, he was pulling ahead in no time, but he stopped short long before we got there. I turned to tease him about being a quitter but his word stopped mine.

"Pa!" That was no greeting. That was a curse.

3

A Visitor

A man stood in the doorway. Walter motioned me behind him and we approached that way.

"What do you want, Pa?" Walter's voice had even less expression than it did earlier, with the people in the village.

"What a way to greet your dear father, Walter! And who's this pretty little thing?" His voice was hoarse and the words slurred. He kept wiping his mouth with the back of his sleeve.

Walter took my arm and led me past his father and into the cabin. His father followed us.

"Yessir! You've got yourself a nice little hidey-hole here, Walter, and a girlie friend to share it with you. Plenty of room for us all. Ah! How lovely! Where's your spirits?"

"Got nothing to drink but water and cider," Walter said.

"Well, cider'll do if it's hard enough. Bring on the cider! My whistle's dry!"

Walter glanced at me, nodded, and went out the

door. I stayed in the corner of the room, trying to disappear.

"Here's your cider, Pa. Good and hard." He hadn't been gone more than a few minutes.

His father grabbed the open jar, which was filled with a liquid the shade of dark honey. I thought about running for help but where would I go? The cider splashed his father's face and the floor before any got to his mouth. He gulped it down. "Ahh! Good stuff! We'll have us a party. Join me!" He stuck the jar in Walter's face.

"No, Pa." Walter turned away.

His father walked over to face him again. "Drink! Take a slug for yourself and then the girl takes some. We take turns, see! It's a party."

"No, Pa." Walter spoke calmly with his arms at his sides.

His father slowly shook his head. "Mr. Perfect," he said as he turned to look around the cabin.

"Where's our pretty little thing?" His father spotted me in a minute. I'd hoped his vision was going with the drink but this was not to be. He moved toward me and the cider jar was at my mouth. I opened my lips just a tiny bit, afraid to put my mouth where his had been but equally afraid not to. I tried to keep from swallowing even a little of the awful stuff. It was terrible. You'd never think that something that tasted as good as sweet cider could turn to this.

His father had no such thoughts, of course, and soon was guzzling more. He sat down at the table, holding the now half-empty jar with both hands. Walter sat down opposite him. I stayed where I was near the door. We each looked around the cabin. Most of the barrels and boxes were open, with stuff spilling out of them. His father must have been searching for drink.

"How'd you find me, Pa?" Walter asked.

His father grinned broadly and took another swallow. "You left a trail, boy. I figured you to be in the valley somewhere. I knew you wouldn't be far from the canal." His grin was smug as he turned to me. "Always a great one for watching them build it, hailing the boats—what few there are!" He turned back to Walter. "The Irish fools that dug it took their wages in shares, most of them. It'll never get beyond Northampton. They won't see a dime for all their work. Serves them Paddies right! Taking away jobs from good American folks. Now they talk of freeing the slaves down South. Soon as they do, those folk'll come and take the rest of the work. Won't be anything left for us decent Americans then."

I'd heard that too. Funny though, you didn't see many towns people lining up for ditch digging—even big ditch digging.

He took another gulp of cider. "Been listening, watching, keeping my eyes peeled every time I came to Granby." Walter's father nodded and went on. "Folks talk. They pay no attention to poor Roy Clark over in the corner. Think I'm too drunk, but I hear a lot. One day I'm in the general store and old lady Sanford tells me to get out and I'm halfway out the door when Mrs. Fisk says to young Dibble, 'And his poor son working so hard delivering wood. Hauls stuff to the mill and back, too.'

"Now I know it's my own dear Walter been gone from home all these months that's living nearby. So I says to myself, says I, 'Best I stay here in Granby a bit and see if I can't find my long-lost son.' And it wasn't but a few days later, there you were coming down the towpath, big as life, and with a dandy little girlfriend right by your side."

We had walked on the towpath to town; that's when he must have seen us. I knew Walter had only used the towpath because I was with him. I glanced at Walter but his face was empty. He was staring at his father.

"I waited till you went in the store and I headed in the direction you'd come from on the towpath. What should I find but this dear little home away from home just waiting for your poor old pa. Knew it was yours when I saw the woodpile. You always pile it the same way. Little Mister Perfect!" He looked up. "You need to stock some liquor, boy. This cider's not hard enough." He shoved back his chair and stood

up and approached some of the still untouched
barrels by the wall.

Walter stepped to the doorway and motioned me to
do the same. Carefully I sidled toward him as his
father whirled around. "Where do you think you're
off to?"

"Just to get you more cider, Pa." Walter's voice was
calm.

"That's a good boy. Bring in all you got. We'll have
ourselves a little—"

I heard no more, for I'd grabbed the cape and I was
out the door. Walter stopped just outside the doorway. "Go out to the privy and wait for me."

"What are you going to do?"

"Get him just as drunk as I can. He'll pass out and
then we'll figure out something."

Spending the night in a privy was not what I had in
mind, but it was a mite warmer in there, sheltered
from the wind. I was grateful again for its tidiness. I
waved my arms around, stamped my feet, and sat
warming my hands in my armpits. I pulled the cape
down around my legs. Then I repeated the actions.
Wave, stamp, sit, pull. Wave, stamp, sit, pull. I don't
know how long I was there before I heard Walter's
soft whistle. He was standing on the towpath.

"Is he out?"

"No," he said just as I heard a crash from inside.
The door opened and Walter's father stood in the

doorway, peering out into the dark. "Where are you, you misbegotten, worthless son of Satan? Get in here! Walter? Walt!"

We stood stock-still and the door banged shut.

"He's ready to start beating up on anybody in reach," Walter said. "With nobody around, he'll just smash things for a while and then he'll pass out."

"Sounds like you've been through this before," I said.

When he didn't answer, I said, "What are we going to do?"

"Find us a barn," he said.

He handed me the scarf and mittens and led off down the towpath. The barn I'd slept in on the way here was too far away. I was afraid of the answer to my next question but had to ask it. "Wilton's?"

Walter grinned. "Time you and Wolf made friends."

By the time we got to the Wilton's place, the wind and cold had gotten way deep inside us. I'd lost the feeling in my fingertips and my feet. I was hoping Wolf was inside the house, but I should have known better. No farmer keeps his watchdog in at night. Sure enough, there was a low growl and the dog came rushing out of the dark toward us. I stepped back and Walter stepped forward. "Hello, Wolf," he said softly. Immediately, Wolf went into his back roll and Walter knelt to scratch his stomach. The dog followed us to the barn and Walter slid back the big barn door just wide enough for us to slide inside. Unfortunately, Wolf came in too. It was so dark in the barn, I couldn't keep track of him, but I could hear his breathing and Walter's frequent soothing murmurs as we felt for hay and bedded down in it, pulling armfuls of it around us. It scratched every bit of skin it could find but it offered warmth and that was very fine indeed. I wrapped my cloak around me and slept.

It seemed only seconds between the time I closed my eyes and the time Walter was shaking my shoulder. I listened for Wolf's breathing but couldn't hear it. In a moment, Walter slid the door open to reveal the still dark sky. It was snowing.

As morning broke, we wordlessly headed back to the towpath and then to the cabin. The wind had died down but the cold was as fierce as ever. The snow was falling more quickly now and it was hard to see the house until we were upon it. The door was open and we approached as quietly as we could, Walter leading the way.

"He's gone!" I whispered.

"Too drunk to go far," Walter said.

The cabin offered little comfort. The fire had long since gone out and it was only slightly warmer inside than out.

We found him in the corner on the floor.

"Passed out, just like you thought, Walter," I said.

He nodded. We built a fire and as it flamed up, we both stared into it for a bit before we began to right the things his father had spilled. Again, Walter seemed anxious that each little thing be placed exactly where it belonged. I was as careful as I could be, but he still realigned everything I touched.

Every so often I'd glance toward his father, but he hadn't moved. At first that was a relief. After a while, it began to be unsettling. I looked at Walter as he watched his father and then walked over to him. He bent down beside him and shook his shoulder. "Pa?" He rolled his father onto his back and said it again, "Pa?" His father's eyes were wide open. With a quick glance in my direction, Walter shook harder and then he put his head down close to his father's face. For a few seconds he stared at him. Then he said, "He's dead." Walter looked at me as if asking me to do something.

"Dead? He can't be dead. He's just drunk. He can't possibly be dead. Shake him again."

Walter just stood there with his head down. "He's dead."

I knelt and, with the tip of my finger, touched his father's hand and drew it quickly away. The flesh was dead cold. Those eyes stared up at the ceiling, seeing nothing. His father's mouth hung open. I stood up, unable to stop my body from shivering.

"How? What killed him?" I cradled my hands in my armpits.

Walter's arms hung straight to his sides. He seemed unable to move. "The drink, I guess."

"Oh, Walter," I said. "I'm so sorry." I moved toward him but he turned away, walking over to stare out the window.

For once I kept quiet. I wished I knew Walter enough to know what to do or say to him now.

The silence stretched on. I thought about my own family and Pa's death and then Ma's death. It was awful to lose your parents. I wondered if Walter was feeling as I had. Town drunk or not, the man was his father.

At last Walter spoke, "One good thing—the misery is over." His voice was thick and he cleared his throat. He turned back to me as if I should say something, but I wasn't sure what.

"Shall I go and get an undertaker?" I asked.

He shook his head. "Can't bring anybody here," he said. "We'll have to bring Pa to town."

He grabbed his coat and headed out the door. "Wait," he said as I took a step toward him.

I backed up against the wall as far away from the body as I could get. I don't know how long I stood there before Walter stepped back inside.

"Where will we bring him?"

"Dunno," he said, "but I want him to have a decent

burial. He wasn't much, but he was my father."

I nodded and went over to the fireplace to tend the fire. I didn't want to look, but every few minutes my eyes wandered over to the corpse on the floor. Finally, Walter went over to the body and put his hands under his father's arms. "Get his feet," he said.

Nothing in me wanted to go near but I took a deep breath and lifted the other end. I was glad I didn't have to get nearer the eyes. As we lifted the body together, I was aware for the first time what the phrase "dead weight" really meant. We half lifted, half dragged the body out the door and around to the corner of the house.

Finally, with both of us out of breath, we laid Walter's father there on the ground. Walter went into the house and came back with a quilt and covered up the body. It was good not to see those awful, staring eyes.

"Now what?" I asked.

"We can't do anything until dark," he said. "Do you know how to skate?"

"Skate!" I said. "At a time like this you ask if I can skate?"

"Can you skate?"

"Yes! I can skate."

"Good," he said. Back to the one-word conversation, apparently.

We left the body and came back inside. I suddenly

realized how hungry I was. Walter was sitting in a chair staring straight ahead; I grabbed a hunk of cheese and some bread. That filled me up in no time. Walter ate some but I'm afraid I consumed most of it. Wherever his thoughts were, they weren't on food.

The rest of the day passed mostly in silence, Walter at one end of the room and I at the other.

When it got dark, Walter stood up. He put on his coat, cap, scarf, and mittens. He nodded when I reached for mine. Then he went to the back of the house and came back with two pairs of skates. He handed them to me and headed toward the frozen canal. I started to follow. "Stay here," he said. "I'll need help."

He came back dragging a long sled.

He drew the sled up beside his father and picked up the top of the covered body. He nodded toward the feet and I reluctantly grabbed them and lifted.

Once the body was on the sled, Walter brought out a long piece of rope and tied it down.

Together we dragged the sled over the snow down to the canal. It tipped a bit going from the towpath to the ice but we managed between the two of us to keep it upright. When the sled was on the ice, we adjusted one pair of skates to fit my shoes and I fastened them on. Fortunately the soles of my boots were strong enough to hold the clamps. Walter had his on in a minute and we set off, dragging the sled behind us.

I did my best to forget that it was a body we were dragging and concentrated on the skating. Walter seemed to prefer no conversation and, for a change, I was happy to oblige. The snow had stopped and what was on the ground was light enough that our skates cut through it easily. The ice beneath the snow was smooth and stretched endlessly in front of us and my feet seemed to remember before my brain did how we'd skated back in Hamden. The sled with its burden scraped effortlessly along behind us. We fell into a rhythm. All thoughts of the cold vanished as we sped down the canal. The towpath on one side and the berm on the other cut out the rest of the world as well as most of the wind, thank goodness. Above us an almost full moon shone through the trees with a bright, white light. We were skating so fast, the tree branches seemed to whip across the moon. Higher up, small clouds did the same.

We were alone with our thoughts and the ice and the moon—and the body.

When we got to a set of locks, Walter whispered, "Shhhh!" as if we'd been chattering away. We both looked to the lockhouse, fearful that someone might be about, but it was all dark. Following Walter's gestures I helped him pull the sled up and then down the towpath on the side away from the house and we snaked it through the rough along the side. Both of us pulled with all our strength, and it seemed like it took hours to go those few yards. When we were well away from the lockhouse we pulled back onto the ice again. Skating seemed like resting after all that work, and it took only seconds to pick up the rhythm again.

Soon the Granby dock appeared. We pulled the sled to shore. "Now what?" I spoke aloud for the first time since we'd hit the canal.

Walter had his skates off and I took mine off as well. "There may be folks about. Stay here." He was up the bank and gone. The skating had warmed me up but in seconds the cold crept back in and I began to shiver. There wasn't a sound but the creaking of some branches in the wind.

"Nobody around," he said when he returned. "We'll take him to the church and leave him at the front door."

"Just leave him there?" I asked.

"Church folks will find him. They'll put him in a crypt or something and bury him come spring."

"Will they do that without knowing who he is?" I asked.

"Oh, they know him," Walter said. "Everybody knows the town drunk. They'll send word to my mother."

It took a lot of strength to drag the sled up the side of the towpath. Going down on the other side was easier. We angled through a field toward the church.

Again our bodies strained against the rope. It would have been easier if we could have used the street instead of the rough, stubbled ground. The street was empty and lamps were on in most of the houses but Walter was being cautious. He kept looking from side to side. Several times he turned completely around. It seemed silly, because nobody would be out in this cold unless they absolutely had to be and apparently nobody did. I decided not to point this out, however. We came around to the front of the church on the side away from the street and we carefully untied the body and lifted it to the step.

"There," Walter whispered, "is the closest my pa's been to a church since the day he was married, I think."

When he moved closer to his father's body, I turned away and walked slowly back to the canal, pulling the now empty sled behind me.

Walter caught up before I got too far. Once back at the cabin, neither of us spoke until I broke the silence before crawling into bed. "Walter," I said. "I'm sorry about your father."

"Eh-yah."

4

The Wood Run

Walter had four potatoes roasting in the fire when I woke up the next morning.

"Walter," I said as I ate more bread and cheese, "what will happen when they find the body this morning?"

He glared at me. "How do I know!" Then he looked down and spoke softly. "There should have been another way. I just don't know what it was."

He drew a deep breath and said, "Wood day."

The abrupt change of subject shook me for a moment. I tried to figure out what wood had to do with his dead father. Walter walked quickly to the fire and put two of the potatoes in his pockets, motioning to me to do the same. They'd help keep us warm for a bit and be our midday dinners.

"Skating's quickest," he said, handing me my skates.

That was fine by me and soon we were speeding down the canal, dragging the empty sled. We skated right by the center of town and stopped in a patch of

woods south of Granby. There was a large pile of
wood all cut into lengths. Walter started piling it on
the sled.

"Won't the person who cut this be mad?" I asked,
grabbing up an armful.

"I cut it," said Walter.

"Whose land is it?"

"Canal corporation."

We brought the wood to the side of the canal near
the town center one sled load at a time before we
were too tired to work any longer.

Then we went back to the woodpile and, with a
glance at me, Walter moved to the side of the pile and
moved three or four logs. It was almost too dark to
see by this time and I was afraid to look, anyway, but
I saw him lift what appeared to be a door in the
ground.

I looked around and then went after him. A root
cellar! Being below the frost level, it was slightly
warmer down here. Things wouldn't freeze. Three
barrels stood against the wall.

"Yours?" I asked. I knew the answer.

"Eh-yah," he said, taking some onions from one
barrel. "Grab some of those apples and potatoes."
He handed me a sack and pointed to the other
barrels.

"What are they for?" I asked.

His look was scornful. "I've had company lately.

Ate up my supply. Don't keep much at the cabin."

"Wouldn't the root cellar be handier closer to where you live?" I asked as I filled the sack.

"Folks might see it. Better this way. Nobody comes here but me."

We loaded the supplies on the empty sled. Walter closed the door and piled logs over it.

"They'll have found the body by now and probably buried it," I said.

He nodded. "Eh-yah."

We skated back to the wood we'd left by the canal and loaded the first of it onto the sled. Walter's knots held as we dragged the load up to the towpath and down again into Granby Center.

I wished Walter would talk more. I wondered what he thought about his father. Did he love him? Had he ever? And what about tomorrow? Surely Mrs. Sanford would have a lot to say about his father being found at the church. I bet she'd love being able to embarrass Walter about his drunken father. His family would have to come down for the funeral or to bring the body back up the mountain to Granville. Was everybody looking for Walter now?

Walter looked around quickly before we stepped into the road but there was no one on the street. We could see people through the windows of the big houses though, in the lamplight.

Motioning me to stay where I was, Walter walked

back toward the church. I began stacking the wood. In a few minutes, he was back.

"Gone," he said. "Somebody found him."

He moved some of the wood I'd stacked into neater rows. When the first load was placed to his satisfaction, we went back for more. This time I watched how Walter had placed the logs and followed his lead as the woodpile grew. Each log end lined up neatly and he made a sort of crisscross pattern at each end of the pile. His father was right. Walter's woodpiles were distinctive.

We were just turning after stacking the last load when Mrs. Sanford appeared behind us. "You're late," she said.

Walter touched his cap as I murmured a good evening. "Yes, ma'am," he said. "Something came up."

"Hmmph!" She was giving no quarter. "A full cord?"

I wondered why she was talking about wood? She should have been saying, "Your father's dead," or even "Guess what we found at the church last night."

Walter nodded.

"We're even then," Mrs. Sanford said, "for now. I'll need more in two weeks. Next time be prompt."

"Eh-yah," said Walter and we left.

Walter went striding off. I ran to catch up. "Your father," I said. "Why didn't she say anything about your father?"

Walter was as baffled as I was. "I don't know," he said. "They must have found him. Seems like she'd have said something."

"What now?"

"Start on the load for the Wiltons."

We pulled the empty sled toward the canal. My shoulders ached. This was hard work. No one was around the Wilton place so we piled the wood at the side of their back door and left.

We headed home, dragging the empty sled behind us. We'd said no more about his father, although it was in the front of both of our minds, I'm sure.

My head was down as Walter's tired footsteps beside me suddenly stopped. One glance at his face led me to look where he was looking.

Someone stood in the open doorway of his house. For a terrifying moment I thought it was his father, but it was a boy who stood there. As we walked closer, the boy spoke "Wah-Wah-Wah-Walter!" It was Jake, and at his feet lay Walter's father.

5

Jake

Walter's face was a series of emotions as surprise fought with anguish. "Jake?"

"Wah-Wah-Wah—" Jake's whole body contorted as he tried to force the words out. His face crumbled as he seemed incapable of saying anything. He kept pointing at the body, but the words wouldn't come.

"Jake," I said. "Whisper."

Walter looked at me as if I'd lost my mind and said, "Whisper?"

I nodded. "Trust me," I said. "You'll have less trouble if you whisper, Jake."

Jake drew a deep breath and his whole body relaxed as his voice fell to a whisper.

"I'm sorry, Walt. It's your father," he whispered.

"I know it's my father." Walter's face showed his annoyance. "How did you come by him?"

Jake let out a breath. "I'm sorry about your father, Walt." He paused, waiting for Walter to speak. When he didn't, Jake whispered on. "I found him first thing this morning. He was lying up against the church. He must have died while trying to get to church, Walt. And nobody was there to let him in."

"And so you decided to bring the body here," I said.

"Well," Jake whispered, then shook his head and went back to a normal tone. "I d-d-didn't know wha-wha-what else t-t-t-to do." He looked at me helplessly.

"By yourself?" I asked.

Jake nodded proudly.

"How?" I asked. My arms remembered how hard it was to lift that body between the two of us. How could Jake have moved it alone?

"Never mind that," said Walter. "How'd you know where I live?"

Jake smiled. "I've known for a long time," he whispered. "I followed you once." He looked toward me and then nodded toward a second sled, wordlessly answering my question.

"Much obliged," Walter said.

It was a cold night, but I suspect the shivers I had were due to the sight we beheld when we drew back the blanket and looked at the body. It seemed different now than it had when we left it at the church. The awful eyes still stared upward, but now the arms were frozen straight out above the head, probably from being dragged by Jake. It made the body seem twice as long as before and more frightening somehow.

"We've got to take him home," Walter said.

"Up the mountain to Granville?" I asked. Walter nodded.

"Of course," Jake whispered.

"We'll have to wait till tomorrow night," Walter said.

We went inside, tired and cold, leaving the body where it lay.

We all worked putting some food together.

"Etta," Jake whispered as we worked, "if I whisper all the time, will I never stammer again?"

I hated to disappoint him. "It only worked some of the time for the Pease boy."

Jake's face fell.

"But," I said, "if you sing the words sometimes, whisper other times, and speak in a real high voice or a very low one, you can usually get by."

Jake grinned. "Like this?" he squeaked.

"See?" I exclaimed. "And even if the voice tricks don't work, go ahead and stammer. We won't mind."

After supper, Jake made for the door. "If you want me to"— he spoke in a deep growl—"I can help you take him up the mountain tomorrow night. Just knock on the wall at the back of the store." He seemed sorry to leave and, truthfully, I was sorry to have him go.

"Might as well spend tonight here then." Walter

threw a glance at me as he said it.

Jake's smile lit up his face. "Fah-fah-fah-fine!"

It didn't take long to fix up a second blanket roll and we all fell asleep quickly.

6

Another Housemate

Jake was gone when I woke up before Walter the next morning. Jake's blanket roll had been dismantled and the quilts neatly folded. When I came back from the privy, Walter was up and cooking. Some of the food had scorched a bit.

"Jake might as well stay here from now on," he said.

"Why?" I said. "He's got a place to live, hasn't he?" Having Jake here wouldn't leave room enough for Bertha and Emory.

"He sleeps on the floor in the back room of the store."

"Well," I said. "It's not the White House but it's a roof over his head. More than some have."

I knew that sounded ungrateful, but what about the others? Again, the time wasn't right to tell Walter my plan.

"I'm asking him today." Walter's voice brooked no room for argument. "I was about to ask him anyway but then you moved in."

"Won't it be crowded?" I asked. My face must have shown how I felt.

"Listen," he said. "Pa found us. Jake found us. Other folks might find us too and if they do come, it'll be better to have three of us here rather than just you and me. That wouldn't look right. Folks would think hard of that." Walter's face was red and he looked down as he spoke.

I was as embarrassed as he was but he was right. A boy and a girl living together wouldn't be looked on kindly. Bertha and Emory coming would put an end to it, but in the meantime it probably was better to have another member of the household—a temporary one, of course. As soon as my family came here, Jake would have to go.

7

Up the Mountain

Jake showed up back at the house just as dark was falling. We bundled up as best we could. It was going to be a long, cold trip up the mountain.

"Ready?" he whispered.

"Almost," said Walter. He had laced Jake's sled to the end of his own to make a double rip. We needed the extra length to support the body's outstretched arms. We carefully secured the corpse to the sleds from head to toe. I tried not to touch it as we worked.

When the body was fastened to the sleds, Walter turned to face Jake. "Jake," he said, "if you don't like where you're living, you can come stay here."

Jake smiled broadly. "Cah-cah-can I br-br-bring Mah-mah-Minerva?"

I guess he was too happy to whisper.

"Cat'd be good, I guess. Keep the mice out." Walter picked up the rope and began to tug the sleds.

I ran back inside to grab the hot potatoes and apples and some quilts. We might not get where we were going by tonight and we'd need food and warmth to keep us from freezing to death on the mountain. With that cheerful thought, I followed the others. The moon had come up and, though it was no longer full, it gave off enough light so that we didn't need to use the lantern Walter had brought.

When we neared the road, Jake ran ahead to scout the territory. He held up his hand for us to stop and, as we did, a sleigh full of people went by.

"Heading for the square dance," Walter said. A square dance sure would have been lots more fun than snaking a dead body up a mountain, I thought, but as usual I kept my thoughts to myself.

In a minute Jake motioned for us to come and we scurried across the road with the sleds.

"Can't we go by the road?" I asked.

Walter shook his head. "Too dangerous."

"Why don't we just leave the body by the church again?" The cold, the dark, and the ghastliness of our errand were giving me second thoughts about our journey.

"Too many folks about tonight, coming and going from the dance. It's better to bring him home. It wasn't right to leave him like that. Should have done this in the first place."

Jake's whistle stopped the talk and we cut through the cemetery and started on up the mountain.

As the way got steeper, it got lots harder. The snow

was deeper in the mountains, with a thick crust on top. Sometimes as we walked on the crust, we'd suddenly break through and be knee-deep in it, the hard top cutting into our legs. Walter and I pulled and Jake shoved the rip from behind for a while and then we switched places.

Then we got to the icy parts. Here the snow was thinner and the ice thicker. Walter had brought his hatchet and several times he had to cut places for our feet to keep us from sliding back. We were between the road and a deep gorge at our left and walking single file with Walter in the lead, when the rope snapped. I screamed and the others gasped as the double rip and its cargo crashed down into the gorge, bouncing against trees as it fell.

For a few minutes we just stood there looking into the darkness where the rip had plunged.

"Wha-wha-what will we do?" Jake's voice shook.

Mine did too as I answered, "We'll have to leave him. We can't get down there."

Walter said nothing. He just started down, running and sliding to the first tree, then on to the next. With a glance at each other, Jake and I followed.

Getting ourselves down into the gorge turned out to be no problem. We struggled to stay upright at first but Jake fell so many times that we soon gave up and just sat down and slid. Saplings slowed our descent. It was darker at the bottom of the gorge, as the moonlight filtered through the trees. As my eyes adjusted to the dark, I could make out Walter standing by the overturned sleds that lay separated on the ground, trailing their ropes. The body was nowhere in sight. Walter lit the lantern and, without a word, we walked around the sleds in widening circles.

I'm not easily spooked, but looking for a dead body in the middle of the night at the bottom of that gorge was scary. I wanted to grab hold of Walter and Jake and get out of there more than anything in the world. The light from the lantern should have helped, but it just made the places where the light didn't shine even darker. I jumped every time I heard anything and the others did too. We jumped at each other's jumping. Nobody spoke, but other sounds came from the woods—branches creaked and snapped, bushes rustled, and the ice on the stream groaned and moaned. You could hear small things scuttling over the crust of snow. In the clear, cold air such sounds were strengthened. The sound of our own footsteps scared us.

As we continued to search for the body, crazy thoughts went through my head. Maybe animals had taken it away. Maybe it had fallen into the stream and been carried away. Maybe Walter's father wasn't dead after all and had somehow thawed out and walked away. Maybe he was hiding behind one of these trees, ready to pounce on us. Maybe something else was.

By mutual unspoken consent we walked in a line as our circle widened. We walked as if the path were made of nails rather than ice, placing each foot gingerly, afraid of what we didn't see. Jake walked so close behind me that he kept treading on my heels; I was close enough to Walter to touch him, although I didn't dare. Suddenly there was a sound like "Ummmph!" and the light went out.

"Walter?" I reached out for him and as I did so, my feet slid out from under me. From my hard seat on the ground I called, "Walter? Are you there?" Crawling on hands and knees, I reached out and grasped a fallen branch as I tried to gain purchase enough on the ice to stand up.

"Eh-yah." His muffled voice came from several steps away. "Knocked the breath from me. I tripped over something."

I could make out Walter a yard or so away as he stood and brushed himself off. The moon came out from behind a cloud, and I looked down at my hand and screamed, snatching my hand away. I stood up, shaking myself all over, especially my hand. That was no branch I'd been clutching so tightly—it was a stiff and frozen arm. It and another bare arm stuck out of the snow bank.

It took a minute for all of us to stop shaking. We

held on to each other as we gasped for air. We didn't even try to talk. After a minute or two, Walter pulled away. Jake and I set about getting the body out. It was hard to deliberately grab hold of that arm again but I did it. As we worked, I heard Walter throwing up over in the bushes. I swallowed the bile in my own throat and held my breath against a smell that hadn't been there when we'd moved the body. By the time Jake and I had freed the body from the snow-drift, Walter was back.

We got the sleds reattached and then pushed and pulled the body back onto, the rip. Jake and Walter retied the ropes and we started up the side of the gorge.

And we thought going up the mountain was hard! The gorge was much, much steeper. We made our way sapling by sapling, with Walter holding on to one with one hand and pulling the sleds with the other as Jake and I pushed. Though I tried not to, my hand kept touching the body and, each time I did so, I gagged or shivered or both. We fell and slipped back many times. By the time we got back up to where the rope had broken, the moon had gone down and it was looking lighter to the east. We were too tired to go another step.

We found a clump of spruce trees that offered some refuge and sat on a log to eat our now stone-cold potatoes and the apples. The sun was almost up.

"How much farther, Walter?" I asked.

"Two miles, more or less."

I looked over at Jake. He was pale and looked about as tired as I felt.

"We're going the rest of the way by the road," I said.

"We can't," said Walter. "There's one farm after another from here on. Folks will be about. They'll see us."

"What if they do?" I was darned if I'd go back near the edge of that gorge. "They're going to know in a while that your father's dead, right?"

Walter nodded.

"So you found your father's body and you're bringing him home for burial. They won't need to know where you live or where you found him. What's wrong with that?"

"Nothing, I guess." Walter admitted. "I was just hoping we'd get to the house, leave the body, and get out of here before anybody saw us. They'd think Pa just died on his own doorstep."

"Wah-Wah-Walt!" Jake said. His voice sunk to a whisper. "Do you really want to leave without talking to your mother?"

Walter looked down for a few minutes. "Not right, is it?" he said. "I just . . . My father . . ." He shook his head. "I don't know how my mother's going to take this."

"All the more reason not to just leave him then," I said. "Better to break the news gently and help her. That's what families do, don't they?"

"Family?" His voice was loud and angry. "Family! A father like that? I don't have any family!" He grabbed up the sled rope and headed for the road.

Even though we had two more steep hills to climb, walking on the road seemed easy after gorge climbing. We did see some people at the farms as we passed, but they were all too busy to pay any attention to three children pulling a double rip up the road.

None of the farms we passed looked very prosperous, but the fourth one we came to was in the worst shape. I knew it was Walter's house before he turned up the drive. A yellow dog raised his head and slowly got to his feet as we pulled into the dooryard. He moved faster when he recognized Walter and came over to him, wagging his tail. Walter patted him. "Hello, Golden," he said. Then he headed into the house, with Golden close behind. Jake and I made no move to follow. No matter what Walter said, this was his family. Families ought to be alone at a time like this.

We stood with the sled at the foot of the steps, which seemed ready to fall off the sill of the house. I turned to Jake. "Do you know Walter's mother?"

"N-n-no," he said. He began to talk in a deep voice.

"Only his father."

The door opened and a woman walked out with Walter behind her. She was tall and very thin and she stood very straight as she looked toward us. She nodded and pulled her plain black shawl tighter against the cold. Her dress was gray and she wore a long white apron. Her hair was brown like Walter's and was pulled back in a bun. She was so thin that her skin seemed stretched tight over her face. Ignoring us, she and Walter walked over to the body on the sled.

"Well, Roy," she said, looking down at the grotesquely positioned body on the sleds. She said no more, only stared down for a while. At last she turned to her son. "It's over then," she said.

Walter nodded.

"He wasn't always like you knew him, Walter." She took a deep breath. "He worked hard and he knew how to have fun. You never heard him play the harmonica or saw him dance because then there was the drink." She paused. "And nothing else."

"You'll need to bury him above ground," she said. "The ground's frozen too hard to dig a grave."

"Eh-yah," he said.

"Put him near the apple tree, Walter. He planted that tree."

They turned and walked side by side back toward the house.

At the door, she turned back to us. "Bring your friends inside, Walter," she said.

Jake and I started to move forward, but Walter said, "No, Ma, not yet." We stopped and they continued on into the house.

After a while, Walter came back. We dragged the double rip to the tree behind the house and, after clearing away the snow, laid the body on a flat place on the ground. Walter led us over to the far end of a stone wall and we began lugging stones from the wall to the body. It was noon or after by the time we'd arranged the stones in tight layers over and around the body. Walter's mother watched from the window as Jake hammered two sticks together for a cross and we propped it up with stones at the head of the makeshift grave.

I thought about my father and then my mother's burial. There were so many tears then. Many people stood beside us at the cemetery in Hamden. Here Jake and I were the sole witnesses. If Walter shed tears, we didn't see them. Walter's eyes were dry as he detached the sleds. I knew we should offer some sort of comfort but I couldn't think of anything to say. We folded up the quilts and tied them to the sleds, then headed back to the house.

Jake and I waited at the step. Walter walked back inside. Through the window I could see Walter and his mother standing close together, talking.

In a few minutes they came out. His mother's face was wet with tears. She stopped at the top of the steps, holding a bow tie quilt.

"Etta and Jake, Ma," Walter said, nodding at each of us in turn.

She nodded back, but her attention was on her son. "You're not staying, are you?" She said this as if she already knew the answer.

"No, Ma," he said. "I can't. I don't want to farm and there's no way for me to make a living up here otherwise."

She handed him the quilt. "And it's too far from the canal." Her smile was sad. "Have you found a place near it?"

"Eh-yah," he said.

"Can you tell me where it is now?" she asked.

"Soon," he said. "I'll be back in a week or so, Ma." She reached up to hold his face in her hands. She looked at him for a minute, nodded, kissed him, and walked quickly into the house.

We took up the sled ropes and walked to the road. When we got there Jake and I looked back at the house but Walter's eyes were straight ahead. His mother stood at the window as we left.

8

Running Out of Room

Jake moved in the next day. He came running up the towpath about noon, slipping and sliding on the ice. He fell twice while we stood waiting for him in the doorway. Each time he fell he got right up again as if nothing had happened and came on at the same breakneck speed. He was carrying a few things in a burlap bag and behind him, running over the ice with a great deal more skill, was a tricolored cat.

Minerva settled in as quickly as Jake did. She made one careful circuit of the room, sniffing each box and corner, and then curled up by the fire. Jake had to get back to his work at the store, but Walter and I spent most of the day resting, worn out from our all-night trip.

I was thinking of where Bertha and Emory could fit in if Jake stayed on when Walter spoke. "I'm going to bring my mother down," he said.

"To live here?"

"Eh-yah."

Well, I could hardly blame him for that. Of course

he wanted his mother with him. Minerva was curled up in my lap, where I'd been stroking her. Now she tensed up and I felt her claws digging into my leg a bit, probably because I'd stiffened up at the thought of yet another person in the tiny cabin. Her purr, now stopped, had been comforting. Walter's words were not. First Jake and now his mother. Where were the rest going to fit?

"Will your mother be willing to live down here?" I asked.

"She can't stay up there. I don't think Pa gave her much to live on but she's lost whatever that was. I can't get to her often enough and there's nobody else. Her own folks stayed away because of Pa."

"What if she doesn't want to come?" I asked.

"If I have to, I can move back to the farm, I guess. We've got to figure out something."

He looked sad at the very idea, but I had all I could do to hold back a grin. He'd said "we" again. I liked that. Whatever his plan was, I was apparently included.

Minerva, convinced the crisis was over, settled back down and resumed her purring. "Why'd you leave the farm in the first place, Walter? Your father?"

"Eh-yah. And I wanted to work on the canal. Pa was right about that. I wanted Ma to come with me then, but she wouldn't leave him."

"Why?"

"I don't know. She said she'd married him for better or for worse. It may have been better once, but there's no doubt that lately it was mostly worse."

It was dark again before Jake came home and we ate our supper of cornmeal mush with maple syrup and apples.

Jake had staked out a corner of the cabin. He fit there fine because he didn't have much to spread out except the bedroll Walter had given him and whatever he had in the bag—a few trinkets and some letters, it looked like.

If each of us took a corner, I supposed we could fit Walter's mother in, but what about Bertha and Emory?

"Are the letters from your family, Jake?" I asked as he came to the table.

"M-m-my m-m-mother," Jake started. I glanced at Walter, who was looking at Jake with interest, waiting patiently for him to get the words out.

Jake picked up his fork and began to eat. "I ca-can hunt pr-pre-pretty good," he said. "Wah-wah-want me to get us some rabbits?"

"That'd be good, Jake," Walter said. "We're running low on meat."

"I'll hunt tomorrow before I go to the store," Jake said.

"Jake, about your mother . . ." I began. I'll admit I was nosy. I wanted to know how come Jake was living with mean old Mrs. Sanford if he had a mother somewhere who wrote to him.

"The-the-this mush is sure good," Jake said.

I can take a hint. I picked up my fork and began to eat.

9

Jake's Story

The next morning there were two rabbits, skinned and gutted, hanging just inside the door when we got up. Jake was long gone and Walter was off too, as soon as he ate breakfast. He didn't ask for my company and I didn't offer it.

I had my own plans. I had to get back in touch with Bertha and Emory. Since they didn't know where I was, they wouldn't be able to get in touch with me. When I was still living in Hamden, we used to meet in Enfield center on the third Sunday of the month. They both had to go to church in the morning but we could usually grab an hour or so to be together in the afternoon. I was farther from Enfield than I'd been in Hamden and on the other side of the river. Getting there would cost money and I thought I knew where to get some.

I grabbed my cape and took some dried apples. Then I put on my skates and started down the canal. As I passed the lockhouse, I looked for signs of habitation but there was no one about. I skated on, enjoying the chance to stretch my legs and my thoughts.

The blacksmith was hard at work as I came into Granby Center. I could hear the bellows and the clang of hammer on metal. A large, gray horse snorted but stood patiently as a new shoe was fitted. Two men stood just inside the large open doorway; they were arguing. One man was finely dressed, the other in farm clothes. I came closer to hear what the cause of the argument was.

"I tell you, that canal's taking water from my land!"

"And I tell you it is not! The water in the canal comes from the river and from feeders." The defender of the canal was as red in the face as the man who confronted him. Both men leaned in so far that their noses were only inches apart. Neither man took any notice of me.

"It takes water from every brook and stream anywhere near it! Damned ditch is nothing but trouble. Jim Hayes can't get to his cornfield."

"He's got a bridge!"

"It's so high and rickety it scares the horses!"

"The canal gives him a market for his corn in New Haven or north to Northampton or any of the towns in between. The boats bring up sugar, molasses, and coffee from the port at New Haven. Someday we'll be able to take it all the way to the Erie and to

Canada."

"Canada! Fat chance! You can't get the corn to New Haven before it rots! Herb Dalton says there's twenty-one locks between here and New Haven."

"It only takes a few minutes to get through each lock! Takes just twenty-four hours to get from Northampton to New Haven."

"Bah! Worse thing ever happened to Granby is that damned ditch!" The farmer strode off. The other man walked back inside the shop. Apparently everybody didn't share Walter's love of the canal. I headed toward the store.

Mrs. Sanford was busy with a customer wanting to barter a crate of chickens. I watched some ladies at the yard good's counter while I waited. Apparently, a new lot of material had come in. Must have come in by the stage, since the canal was frozen. They were holding pieces of fabric across their chests and arms and chattering about collars and dress styles.

When her customer had gone at last, Mrs. Sanford turned to me. "Yes? What is it?"

"Do you have shoe tops for stitching?" I asked.

"I do." Wouldn't you think she'd at least smile?

"How much do you pay apiece?" I'd be as businesslike as she was.

"Five cents for perfect ones."

"What do you pay if they're not?" I thought to make a little pleasantry. I should have known better.

"Not a penny!" she said and turned away in disgust.

"Wait a minute—I was just joshing," I said.

"I've no time to waste on foolishness," she said.

"I'd like to do some shoe tops," I said as solemnly as I could, "and I'll do them perfectly. Give me five of them."

"I'll give you one kit," she said, "and it'll be the only one you'll ever see if I don't get it back by store closing with every stitch perfect."

"Done and done!" I said. She handed me the pieces of cut leather and a small spool of black thread.

"What about needle and thimble?" I asked.

She slapped both down on the counter. "Fifty cents," she said.

"So, to make five cents, I spend fifty?" I asked.

"That's the price. Take it or don't. It's all the same to me," she said.

I took it and gave her my last fifty cents. Ten tops would repay my investment.

"Where are you staying?"

"With friends."

"Where's Jake living?" she asked, without releasing the kit.

"Jake?" I asked as innocently as I could. "Is he the boy who works here?"

"Don't give me your sass, young lady," she said. She released the kit to shake a finger at me. "Jake's parents are under the impression that he lives safely here with me. When they find out that he is not, and they shall for I will tell them as soon as possible, they will not be pleased!"

"Where are his parents? Why doesn't he live with them?"

"Mr. and Mrs. Whittingham are Shakers and live in the community at Enfield," she said with a sniff.

Shakers! I'd heard about them. People said they had fits and danced in church. I wasn't sure about the fits but dancing in church seemed better than sitting there for hours while the preacher droned on. Still, it was peculiar.

"When things didn't work out, Jake came to live with me. Now, he slips off at night and sleeps somewhere else. I need to know where that is," she said.

"Isn't he here?" I said. "Let's ask him."

"He's fetching yarn from the carder mill," she said. "And I have asked him, but he won't answer. Pretends he can't get the words out. If he's off with you and Walter, there'll be trouble. You mark my words."

"I will," I said. "Consider them marked." I picked up the kit and hurried out.

So Jake's parents were Shakers. They must have gone to live in the Shaker community after Jake was born, because Shakers didn't believe in having children. I knew that. You couldn't be born a Shaker;

you had to become one.

There were boys skating on the canal as I approached it so I stayed on the towpath. That left me visible to people from the road if they happened to be looking this way. I didn't see anybody, but I kept looking over my shoulder as I headed home. I was worried about Mrs. Sanford. Would she follow me? Was she that nosy? Several times I turned quickly, hearing a snap behind me, but there was no one there. Trees will snap like that sometimes when a cold spell lets up.

The shoe top was all cut and punched. It just had to be stitched together. Somebody else's job was to sew them on to the bottoms. They didn't give you much extra thread and I had to start over a couple of times until I figured out which seam to do first, but I had it done and back to Mrs. Sanford before closing.

She took it over to the light to make sure I'd done it right and she looked like she was in pain when she handed me the five cents.

"I'll take ten more," I said, and she definitely winced as she handed me ten kits.

That evening I could hardly wait for the rabbit stew to be dished out before I started in on Jake.

"How long have your parents been Shakers, Jake?" I figured I might as well plow right in.

He dropped his spoon. Walter's head shot up.

"Hah-hah-how d-d-did ya-ya-you know?" Jake's

stammer was back in full force.

"Mrs. Sanford," I said.

"That busybody!" Walter said. "Has to tell all she knows."

"I—I—it's all right." Jake began to whisper. "I was going to tell you anyway."

He sipped some stew broth. Then he spoke in a high, squeaky voice. "My mother and father decided to go with the Believers when I was six."

"I thought they were Shakers," I said.

"Those *are* Shakers," he whispered. "They call themselves United Society of Believers in Christ's Second Coming," he said, "but most nonbelievers call them Shakers."

"Because they shake and fall down in fits," I said.

"They dance and they sing with the spirit," he corrected, this time singing the words. He was enjoying all those voice changes.

"But they don't have any fun," I said. Some of what I knew about the Shakers had to be true.

"They do too have fun," he said. "At least some of them do. They work hard but they laugh and sing a lot."

"They hate children," I said. "That's why they don't have any."

"Wr-wrong again." Jake was beginning to grin now. He spoke in a deep voice. "Men and women live apart in the dormitories. They don't have babies, but they take in lots of orphans, and some folks, like mine, come with their children. The whole community cares for them. They teach them their letters and a trade if they stay long enough."

Walter hadn't looked up from his supper, but he was listening, all right. I wondered if he knew the answers to my questions or was learning this for the first time like I was.

"So why didn't you stay if it's all so nice in there? Were they mean to you?"

"No, they weren't mean." Jake's face was sad again. "It's just that when your mama and papa live in different parts of the place and hardly even see each other, they don't seem like your parents anymore. It's hard. You're not supposed to be with them any more than with the others, so it's all different. I wanted to leave. Seemed easier somehow." He'd forgotten to speak in a crazy voice but his words were coming out fine. Seemed like sometimes, when he didn't think about it, the stammering went away by itself.

"So you ran away," I said, "in the middle of the night."

Walter grunted. Jake was laughing hard now. "No," he said. "I asked for a meeting with the elders and told them I wanted to go. So they found me a place with Mrs. Sanford."

"And you'll never see your poor mother and father

again," I said.

"I can see them whenever I go over to Enfield," he said. "And sometimes Pa brings the seed to the store and we talk awhile then. He brings letters from Ma and takes mine. It isn't the way it used to be, but it's all right." He looked around the cabin and smiled. "Going to be better now," he said.

My version was a bit more exciting but, when I thought about it, Jake's version was better for him, at least.

"Does your father ever get to Somers or Stafford Springs?" I asked.

"I don't know," Jake said. "Someone from the community does, I bet. They sell seeds most everywhere. Why?"

"Could he get some letters to those places?"

"I guess so. Got some?"

"Not yet," I said, "but I will tomorrow."

I finished two shoe tops that evening and then I began to write my letters. I was in the middle of the second letter when a rock came through the window.

10

Attacked

The rock landed about two feet from where I sat, and for a second or two we all just stared at it as it lay on the floor surrounded by the broken shards of glass. Then another window shattered and another rock bounced into the room.

"Get down!" I yelled, and we all dove for cover. Walter reached up from his place on the floor and blew out the lamp. He crawled over to the window to peer outside.

"Can you see anyone?" I asked.

"Nope. Too dark," he said.

We could hear them, though. There was a lot of yelling from the woods. Loud crashes continued as things bounced against our walls and door.

Jake had crawled over to the door and taken his rifle from its place against the wall.

"Is it loaded?" I whispered. Jake's gun was a cap-and-ball muzzle loader. It would take time to load.

"Yep!" he said.

Walter was back beside us. "Well, don't use it yet,"

he said. "Not unless you have to. Let me see what I can see."

On his hands and knees, Walter crept back over to the door and eased it open. Another thud came from the wall nearest me. I could see Walter in the starlight of the open doorway. In a minute the door closed and he was gone. Almost as quickly, someone yelled and another rock smashed against the door.

Then Walter was back.

"Where's your black powder, Jake?" he whispered.

"In a bag in my corner." Jake was already crawling toward it.

"Etta," Walter said, "when I open the door, you go sixty yards toward the road. Stay low and move fast. Get behind a tree and wait till you hear me yell. Then tell us to fire in the loudest, deepest voice you've got."

Jake was back with matches and his powder bag.

Walter took them. "Jake," he said, "go about sixty yards directly left. Wait till you hear me and Etta yell, then fire your gun in the air and make a lot of noise."

"Who are they?" I asked.

"River boys," he said, and we were out the door.

A rock crashed above my head as I ran to the woods. It was cold but I was too scared to think about that. I have no idea how far I ran. Who could measure sixty yards at a time like that? I wouldn't have been able to do it in daylight. At night, scared half out of my wits, there was no chance. I ran till I came to a big tree and hid behind it. Crashing noises kept coming from the house and there were voices out to my right.

Then I heard Walter yell, "There they are!"

Suddenly his voice seemed to be coming from everywhere, with cries of "Get 'em!" and "There's one behind the tree!"

I lowered my voice as deeply as I could and shouted, "Fire your weapons!"

I heard Jake yell, also in a deep voice, "After them, men!" from the other side of the house. This was followed by the blast of a gun. Immediately, the sky lit up as the whole woods over Walter's way appeared to be on fire. The noise of people crashing though the underbrush was almost immediate. It grew fainter and then there was silence.

"All clear, general. You too Mr. Whittingham!" Walter said with a laugh, and we walked back toward our battered home.

We were cleaning up the mess on the floor when I asked, "Who were they?"

"River boys," said Walter.

"Boys who live in the river?" I asked.

"They're boys hired by the river ports like Springfield, Hartford, and Middletown on the Connecticut to do damage to the canal. In the spring and summer they fill in parts of the feeders or make the canal embankments collapse. In the winter they damage the buildings and pile rocks in the locks."

"Why?"

"Because if the canal gets working good, those river cities will get less traffic, or they think they will."

"How does throwing rocks at us hurt the canal?"

"It doesn't," he said, "but they don't know that."

"Th-they mu-must have seen the lights and thought we were canal workers," Jake said.

We were tacking bags over the broken windows when Walter said, "You know, perhaps it's time we were."

"We were what?" asked Jake.

But my mind had been working too. "Canal workers," I said.

"Whe-whe-we're just children!" he said.

"And so are the river boys," said Walter. "If they can be hired, so can we."

"I du-du-don't want to do damage," said Jake.

"We won't," I said. "We can prevent it. We can be watchdogs."

11

The Challenge

The next morning Walter and I set off on skates down the canal to Simsbury. Jake had debated for a long time whether or not to come with us. He wanted to, but eventually he decided that he'd better go on working at the store until we had something definite lined up. Besides, he had my letters for his father. I could have used the post, of course, but that meant leaving the letters with Mrs. Sanford, and I didn't want to do that. I hadn't made any promises in those letters, but I'd told Bertha and Emory I'd see them in Enfield in two weeks. I did tell them that things were looking very promising.

This time, when we got to the lockhouse near Granby, Walter and I took off our skates and looked around. Jake hurried on to the store. Walter said that the Chapman family had lived in the lockhouse through the fall, but no one was living there now. From what we could see, it looked to be in pretty sad shape. The river boys had managed to smash all the windows. There were big holes in the floor and some

of the dark green clapboards were badly damaged.
There was no outhouse; probably the boys had
carried it away. The pump had been torn off the well
and lay strewn around in pieces. Still, the lockhouse
had been more sturdily built than our little cabin and
there were five rooms besides the summer kitchen.

"Fixable," said Walter with a grin.

"Fixable," I said, and we put our skates back on
and went on to Simsbury, seven miles south on the
canal.

It was late morning by the time we entered
Simsbury Center. The town was bigger than Granby,
and lots of folks were about, shopping or just visit-
ing. Many were quite stylishly dressed. It took a
minute to spot the little yellow building over by the
church with the sign above the door that read THE
NEW HAVEN AND NORTHAMPTON CANAL COMPANY.

Walter gave me a thumbs-up sign and we went
inside. We really hadn't discussed what we would
say. Maybe Walter had a plan, but I sure didn't. I figured the situation would decide that for us.

A man sat at a large desk covered with papers on
one side of the room. His gray hair was mussed and
he roughed it more with his hand as he looked at his
account book. As we entered he looked up. "Yes,
what is it?"

"We'd like to talk about a job."

He was already back into the account book.

Without looking at us he said, "I don't have any jobs to offer. All the towpath jobs are filled."

"We don't want towpath jobs," I said. "We're thinking more along the lines of security."

Without removing his eyes from his task, he said, "We don't have security jobs on the canal."

"Well, that's our point," said Walter. "You should. The lockhouse in Granby has nearly been destroyed by river boys."

"And," I added, "one of the other canal buildings has been vandalized as well."

Walter shot me a warning look, but I didn't think that this man was about to ask us which other house.

"Maybe so," said the man, "but we can't afford a security force and, if we could, it wouldn't be children we'd be hiring."

"We can protect the lockhouse," I said.

"I thought you said it was nearly destroyed," he said. This time at least he looked up. Still, he didn't seem impressed by our presence, more shocked at our nerve, I think.

"Eh-yah, it was," said Walter. "It should be fixed up and we can do that. You don't want canal property to be seen in such a shambles when the traffic starts up this spring. Folks need to see this as a modern enterprise. There's too much talk about its failing."

"This hire won't cost you much," I said, "just the

use of the house."

"Just what is it that you think you can do in return
for the use of a lockhouse?"

"We'd patrol the canal from Granby to the
Massachusetts line. Keep it free of vandalism."

"It'd take more than two children to do that," he
said. "Those river boys are tough."

"We fought off a gang of them last night," I said.
"Must have been twenty thugs out there and we
chased them off." Walter was suddenly overcome
with a spell of coughing.

"Chased them off from where?" he said.

"From one of the foreman's houses," I said.

"Can you prove it? Do you have witnesses?"

"Eh-yah," said Walter. "Jake Whittingham saw the
whole thing."

"How old is Jake Whittingham?"

He would have to ask that. "Ten," I said softly. I
knew we were sunk.

"Sorry," said the canal man. "You'll have to come
up with better evidence than the testimony of three
children."

I turned and started out of the office, but Walter
stood his ground.

"If we can get you that evidence," he said, "can we
make a deal?"

"If you can bring me real evidence that would serve
in a court of law." The man's tone showed how sure

he was that this would never happen. "We might have a deal then."

"My name is Walter Clark and this is Etta Prentice," said Walter, holding out his hand. "And your name, sir?"

"John Edmonds," he said, rising to shake Walter's hand with a disbelieving grin.

"Pleased to meet you, Mr. Edmonds," said Walter. "You'll be hearing from us soon."

With that, we turned and left the canal office.

Outside, the sun was warm and we sat on the church steps to enjoy it.

"Any ideas?" I asked.

"None yet," he said, "but we'll come up with something."

We spent the rest of the day looking around Simsbury Center, each lost in our own thoughts. If we could do it—get the lockhouse for a home—my dream of getting my family together again under one roof would be within reach. With all those rooms, Walter would surely let me get Bertha out of the mills and Emory off the farm to live with us. Between us all, we could sew enough shoe tops to support ourselves.

When the sun neared the horizon, we put on our skates and headed back to Granby.

That night after supper, Minerva took up roost on Jake's lap and we sat around the table trying to figure out what we could do.

"We need to capture one of the river boys," I said, "and take him to Simsbury. The damage to the lock-house will be added proof."

"Eh-yah," said Walter, "but how are we going to do that? Those boys I saw last night are bigger than me and probably stronger than all three of us put togeth-er."

"N-n-next time they come," said Jake, "we'll pick out the weakest one and tackle him. Then, Walter, you and I can hold him while Etta runs to get the constable."

"And while you're trying to do that," I said, "those other river boys will be on you like a shot and you'll lose your captive and, probably, your lives as well."

"The-the-then we'll trap him," said Jake. "We'll set up a spring trap and swing him up by the leg."

"And the other boys will come back and beat us up and get him down," I said.

"Do they always come in a gang?" he asked.

"Most times, I think." Walter got up to poke the fire.

"How many were there last night?" Jake asked.

"Dunno," said Walter. "More than five—maybe eight. Course, according to Etta there were twenty."

I laughed. "Well, maybe I stretched it a bit. We can do it, though; all we need is a plan."

Walter shook his head. "A plan and the strength of twenty."

12

The Trap

Spring was already in the air. It wouldn't be long before the canal opened for traffic. With the frost out of the ground, it would be easier for the river boys to damage the canal with cave-ins and other deviltry. If we were going to do something, we had to do it soon.

I kept stitching shoe tops and Walter worked some at the Wiltons and delivered wood. Every chance he had, he'd walk down to the canal. Jake went on with his store job, but each night after supper, we'd put our heads together and plan. So far, we'd come up with some pretty wild and funny ideas, but nothing that we thought would actually work.

It was during a trip to Walter's root cellar for onions and carrots that it hit me.

"Walter," I said, "here's our trap."

He grinned at me from over the potato sacks. "Oh it's a fine trap. All we have to do is get the river boys to run through this spot in the middle of nowhere when the root cellar door is open."

"All we need is one river boy," I said.

"There's no reason for him to be here. It's not even close to the canal."

"Then we build a new root cellar that is."

"Where would you build it?"

"One step in front of a running river boy," I said.

Walter laughed. "If we can just get him to stand there with his foot in the air while we dig it."

We were both laughing now, but I still thought that I'd hit on a plan.

After supper that night, we worked on it.

"If you were a gang of river boys and you wanted to do your first spring damage, what would you hit?" I asked Walter.

"The locks," he said.

"Which locks?"

"Ones near a damaged lockhouse," Walter said, "where they wouldn't have to worry about folks chasing them off. They probably know there's no one living in the lockhouse near Granby Center."

"But they know or they think they know that a lot of men with guns are close by," I said. "Remember, we scared them so much they haven't been back this way, and I haven't seen any further damage at the locks or the lockhouse. Have you?"

"No," he admitted. "Serves us right for being so clever."

"There's another set of locks just north of Simsbury," said Jake. "Wha-what shape is that lockhouse in? Anybody living there?"

"We passed right by those locks on the way to
Simsbury, but we didn't think to look at that lockhouse. Tomorrow's Sunday," Walter said. "Let's go
find out."

We set off at daybreak. Minerva followed for a
while but got distracted at a hollow tree. It was
nearly noon when we got to the locks at Simsbury
even though we walked on the road from Granby
south. This lockhouse was in better shape than the
one near Granby, although you could tell the vandals
had been there. There was some furniture inside, but
much of it was broken. The windows were smashed
and somebody had piled rocks on the ice at the first
lock. A little more melt and those rocks would fall to
the bottom. Since the water was only about four feet
deep, it wouldn't take many rocks to make the lock
impassable. It looked like the shafts on the locks
were bent as well.

Jake started to move the rocks but Walter stopped
him. "Leave them, Jake. We don't want anybody to
know we've been here."

We walked around the house, surveying the
territory.

"Here's where the root cellar goes," said Walter,
pointing to a flat area at the side of the lockhouse
fairly close to the lock.

"Only trouble is," I said, "by the time the ground's

soft enough to dig a root cellar, the canal will be open and it might be too late."

"Better start now, then," Jake said.

"Jake, we don't even know we can stay here yet," I said.

"Oh, whe-whe-will," he said. "N-n-nobody will be able to k-k-keep both you and Walter from doing what you've a mah-mah-mind to do. If you want this lah-lah-lockhouse, sooner or later you'll have it."

He began gathering up wood for a fire. Walter and I joined in and, as soon as we had enough wood, we lit a fire on the frozen ground where our root cellar/trap was to be.

Walter found a shovel inside the lockhouse and we began the slow work of building a fire in one spot, letting it burn awhile, then rebuilding the fire a couple of feet over. We put Jake to building the fires because Walter took too long placing the logs just so. Where the fire had been, we dug as deep as we could, which wasn't far, before we hit frozen ground and had to stop. Our fires were only about a foot down when it got dark and we had to quit.

We'd brought quilts, potatoes, and apples, and we picked out spots on the floor of the lockhouse. It was hard comfort but we were so tired, we fell asleep almost immediately.

The next morning we were at it again. Minerva showed up soon after sunrise.

We got down below the frost line by noon and could stop building the fires. Things went quicker then. We took turns with the shovel and finally had a pit that was eight feet deep, ten feet long, and about five feet wide. It would make a fine root cellar. Would it also make a good trap? We sloped the ground at the nearest end where the steps would go and then filled the whole thing in with brush before we spent another night on the lockhouse floor.

"Mrs. Sanford will be mad that you missed work," I said to Jake the next morning as we broke camp.

"It's not worth the little she pays me putting up with her tongue-lashing much longer," Jake answered. "I'll quit as soon as we've got something going."

"What about your father?" asked Walter.

"Saw him Friday," said Jake. "I gave him your letters, Etta, and told him I was living with Walter."

"How'd he take it?" I asked.

"Like a Shaker," he grinned. "He said he hadn't realized how bad it was with Mrs. Sanford, but I don't know how happy he is that I'm living with you and Etta. I didn't tell him how old you are. He'll find out soon enough. What's the next step, Walter?"

"I think we've got to move house," he said.

"Why?" I asked.

"I can't bring my mother to a shack."

"Walter," I said, "where will we go? We can't hide

out in the lockhouse. It's too close to the road and a lockkeeper will be moving in soon."

"I dunno," said Walter. "But we've got to come up with something and soon."

13

Letters

I was getting to the point where I could sew ten shoe tops in a day and still have time to do some fishing in the lakes at Congamond. Jake went on working at the store and Walter got his boat out and began making deliveries up and down the canal. There was still too much ice for the bigger canal boats, but his rowboat could maneuver around it.

I hoped my letters had gotten through to Emory and Bertha. I needed to know that they'd be there in Enfield on Sunday for it was going to take some doing for me to get there now that I was so much farther away.

Then, just in time, Jake came back with letters for me from both of them. I rushed to open Emory's first:

> Dear Etta,
>
> Five ewes have lamed with two to come. We have three new calfs. I will see you in Enfield next Sunday.
>
> Emory

Who cared about the sheep and the calves? He'd said

nothing about my steps toward getting our home together. Well, Emory was young and not much good at writing. We'd see each other Sunday. We'd talk then and I could tell him all about his new home.

Perhaps Emory could get a job on the towpath. According to Walter, those boys have a fine life. They walk the horses or mules or ride them thirty miles one way and then come back towing in the other direction. That way they're never more than thirty miles from home. Emory loved animals and was good with horses. What a nice life for Emory that would be. Of course, I'd have to be sure that he had a decent place to stay when he was at the other end. I'd put tasty food in his dinner pail. I was so occupied thinking about how nice I could make life for Emory that it was a few minutes before I opened Bertha's letter.

Dear Etta,

How surprised I was to get your letter from a Shaker! He was standing at the gate of the mill last evening when I came out. At first I thought he was looking to convert me. No chance of that!

I have wonderful news! All the girls on my line got a raise. I now make $8.50 per week. From that, of course, I have to pay board and room but that still leaves me $2.50 for my very own. I've got more responsibilities but I

can handle it just fine. I never have told them
my age. It's lucky I'm tall.

I look forward to seeing you and Emory on
Sunday in Enfield.
Your loving sister,
Bertha

Why, that letter was almost happy. Leave it to
Bertha to make the best of a bad situation. I'd always
felt like the big sister even though she was older than
I. Bertha was too busy having fun. Back home she
was the one who was always in trouble for not doing
her work. Now she was doing nothing but work.
She'd be really happy to get out of that awful mill
and into the sunshine.

Walter and Jake were stacking wood when I finally
came back inside. Without looking up, Walter said,
"Your supper's there." He pointed to a covered dish
by the fire and then went back to his work.

14

Enfield

Getting to Enfield was easier than I thought and it
didn't cost a penny. Jake set us up with Zephaniah
Brown, a peddler who was on his way to Enfield for
new supplies and was willing to take us along.
Apparently, Jake had often traveled with him. They
greeted each other like old friends.

"Top of the morning, Jake," the peddler called out
cheerfully when we met him in Granby Center. It was
just barely the top of the morning—the sun had not
yet risen. Zephaniah wore a peddler's cap and was
dressed in well worn but quite respectable clothing.
His old horse, Ned, was obviously well cared for. As
we approached, Zephaniah was feeding him a carrot
and stroking his face.

Zephaniah had a load of shoe tops to take to
Enfield and, as we helped him load the peddler's cart,
I wondered how many of them I had sewn. They
were piled high in the cart when we climbed up to sit
beside Zephaniah and set off from Granby. Of
course, the cart held more than the shoe tops. It was

fitted out with a series of cabinet doors that opened to reveal thread, yarn, needles of all kinds, ax heads and other tools, fishing tackle, and ladies' collars and buttons—anything a farmer and his family might need. Each item had its place on door or shelf.

Zephaniah Brown turned out to be a pleasant man who knew every farm and shop from Granby to Enfield, as he'd traded with most of them. As we clopped by each farm, he filled us in on the place and the families who lived there. The old horse moved slowly, not much faster than I could walk. Even so, it was lots more pleasant and less tiring than hiking over by myself. We crossed the Connecticut on the ferry (Zephaniah paid the fare) and got to Enfield well before noon. I said goodbye to Zephaniah and Jake at Enfield Center and they went on to the Shaker Village.

All the shops were closed, it being the Sabbath, so I sat down by the river and waited for Bertha and Emory.

It was early afternoon before Emory showed up. He jumped off the wagon before it even stopped to let him off, turning back to yell, "Thank you, Mr. Evans. I sure appreciate the ride." The farmer waved, slapped the reins, and moved on.

Emory and I ran toward each other and just hung on for a while. It felt so good to hug him again. When I finally pulled back to look at him, I was shocked at how he'd grown.

Wiping away glad tears, we sat on the steps of the general store to talk and wait for Bertha.

"Etta," he said. "I was so glad to get your letter. I'd been really worried about you."

"How are the Evanses treating you, Emory?" I asked. "Are they mean?"

"No," he said, patting my hand. "The Evanses are real good to me, Etta. I've got my own room and everything. They haven't any children of their own."

I looked him over carefully. He was dressed well enough: broadfall jean trousers and a dark brown waumas. Lots of men and boys wore those now instead of a coat in the winter. His boots were good.

"But they work you from morning to night, don't they" I said. "It's like being a slave, isn't it?"

Emory laughed. "Everybody works hard on a farm, Etta. They don't make me work any harder than they do themselves. You should see the new calves, Etta," he went on excitedly. "Mr. Evans is going to keep them all. So I get to help raise them. Think of it, Etta! Three calves! And he's letting me plant a piece myself this year. We're going to stop on the way home at the Shaker Village for some seed." His face was so full of smile you could scarcely see his eyes.

"That's wonderful, Emory!" I tried to sound excited and pleased but I really didn't care the least bit about cows or gardens. I let him go on and on while we waited for Bertha. I tried to make my face look interested. I was surprised that he looked so well. His cheeks were rosy and he'd put on weight since I had seen him last fall. At least they must be feeding him enough.

A large carriage drew up to the center drawn by a team of horses. The door opened and a bunch of girls scrambled out. They were chattering and fussing with their bonnets and cloaks. They began to move toward the river when one, dressed all in blue, detached herself from the rest and came toward us.

"Awwkk!" I cried. "Bertha!"

She grinned and then opened her arms and ran toward us. Emory and I ran too, meeting her in a hug that nearly knocked her over.

"Gosh, Bert," said Emory. "You look like a fine lady."

"Like my outfit?" she asked, pulling away and twirling all the way around. Her petticoats swirled way out. "I just got it in Stafford. Oh, it's nice to wear something that wasn't cut down."

She pulled back her cloak so we could see the dark blue wool dress. It had close-set hooks and eyes from the waist to her throat. The long sleeves put the fullness well below her elbows in the latest fashion. There was lace trim along the piping. She was wearing stays that made her waist a little higher. Her skirt ended just above her ankles with considerable flare. Her stockings were fine and dark blue to match the dress. Her bonnet was quilted and trimmed with lace.

In my day cap, shawl, and plain wool frock, I felt like a country cousin.

"Goodness, Bertha," I said. "How many petticoats are you wearing?"

"Four," she giggled. "Do you like it?"

"It's beautiful," said Emory with a grin. "You're beautiful."

"Thank you, Emory," she said, hugging him again. Then she looked toward me. "Etta?" she said hesitantly.

"You look fine, Bertha," I said. I couldn't begrudge her that. "You should have nice clothes. Heaven knows you work hard enough for them."

"Thanks, Etta." She looked relieved. "I do work hard. But things are getting better at the boarding-house. We get lessons three nights a week now. Men come and teach us literature and writing and our sums. They're from the church. They do a prayer service and then we get to the lessons."

We walked over and sat on the steps at the general store. Emory and Bertha talked on and on about farms and factories. It was just so good to hear their voices and to be with them that I didn't care what they talked about. I would gaze at Emory for a while, then I'd turn and watch Bertha. I really wasn't listening to anything they said, just enjoying being with them at last. Finally, it was my turn to talk.

"I think it will be soon," I said. I grinned and sat back to wait for their reaction.

"What will be soon?" Emory asked. Bertha just looked at me.

"Our home, silly," I said. "What we've been working for. I think we'll have our home again soon."

"Where?" They both asked at once.

Then I told them all about Walter and Jake and the cabin and the canal. It took a long time because there was so much to tell.

When I got to the part about losing Walter's father's body in the gorge, Emory's eyes were huge. He spoke for the first time since I'd begun my tale. "Weren't you scared, Etta?"

"I was terrified," I said. "It was the creepiest, scariest thing I've ever done."

"Gosh!" he said. "What a great story! I believe Henry Ashford will like that one." He answered my unspoken question. "He lives at the next farm. He tells good stories like you do, Etta."

"It's not a story," I said. "It's the truth."

"Best kind of story," he said. Bertha laughed and hugged him.

Shaking my head, I went on with the rest of it. I ended, finally, with "So, you can see that it shouldn't be much longer before we can be a family again!" I waited for their reaction to this great news.

"I thought we were a family now," Emory said. "I'm still your brother, aren't I?"

"Oh, Emory," I said. "Of course, you'll always be my brother, but families should live together. Remember how it used to be?"

"How far away is Granby?" Bertha asked.

"A little over ten miles," I said.

"I'd have to leave the mill," she said.

"Well of course you'd leave the mill! That's the best part! You get to work outdoors instead of in that awful, dangerous place," I said. "We'll find work with the canal."

"Doing what?" she asked.

"I don't know what yet," I said. "But think of it, Bertha. You can hop on a boat and get to New Haven or Northampton in no time. Walter says the boys just jump down on the packet boats from the bridges and they let them ride anywhere they want to."

"Jump from a bridge?" she said. "That's all right for boys, but it sounds very unladylike."

"Unladylike?" I said. I looked at her with amazement. "Bertha, it's me, Etta! We climbed trees together, swam in the pond behind the house like boys did. Don't talk about ladylike to me! We were never ladylike unless they made us be."

"But that was years ago," she said. "When we were little."

Emory got us back to the subject. "Would it be before next year?"

"Oh, Emory," I said. "I hope so. I surely do hope so."

"I'd kind of like to see the calves grow up," he said. "I'd like to plant that garden."

Suddenly I knew what the trouble was. They hadn't seen it. They needed to see the cabin and the way we'd fixed it up. They needed to see the canal. They needed to meet Walter and Jake.

"You've got to come," I said. "You've got to come for a visit. Then you'll see how it can all work out."

"I'd like that, Etta," said Emory. "I'd like to see where you live."

"Bertha," I said. "Can you get time off from the mill?"

"I don't know," she said. "They fire girls for not showing up. They even fire you for being five minutes late sometimes. You have to be in the boardinghouse by eight each evening. How could I do it? I don't want to lose my job."

If things worked out, she'd be quitting her job anyway, but I could see why Bertha was worried.

"How about family?" I said. "They must give people time off to take care of family business— people die, get sick, you know."

"Maybe," she said. "Maybe I can work something out with one of the bosses. I'll let you know."

Before long the farmer came back to get Emory. "Come and meet Mr. Evans," Emory said. He grabbed my hand and Bertha's. We walked with him over to the wagon.

"Mr. Evans," he said. "These are my sisters, Bertha and Etta."

Mr. Evans smiled and tipped his hat. "I'm pleased to meet you both. We think a lot of young Emory here."

"He's worth a lot," I said. "You be good to him."

Emory was embarrassed at my bold speech, I think, but Mr. Evans didn't bat an eye.

"We try to be," he said. "Hop aboard, Emory, it's getting toward milking time."

Emory hugged us both and climbed onto the wagon. "See you soon. Write to me," he called, and he waved as they drove off.

"He looks good," said Bertha. "Seems happy too."

The girls Bertha had ridden in with were all coming back from their river walk. Bertha introduced me to most of them but I quickly forgot their names. One of them had her arm around Bertha's waist as they walked over to their carriage, which had stopped down the street. Bertha joined right in with them, forgetting me entirely. Then just before she stepped into the carriage, she turned and ran back to me.

"Oh, Etta," she said. "Don't look so sad. It'll be all right. Really, it will." I brushed away tears and hugged her. "I'll find a way to visit you soon." Then she turned and ran to the carriage before I could say another thing. In a minute they were all inside. The door shut. The driver slapped the reins and they were gone.

15

The Deal

"It's time to make things legal," Walter said after breakfast the next morning. "I'm going back to see Mr. Edmonds at the canal office. You coming?"

"I dunno," I said. "What are you going to see him about?"

"If the river ports hire boys to do damage to the canal," he said, "we ought to be able to talk Mr. Edmonds into hiring us to prevent them from doing it."

"We tried that," I said. "He wasn't interested."

"Then we'll try it again," said Walter, "with new arguments."

Jake said, "Can we stop at Mrs. Sanford's store?"

"Why?" I said.

"If it's hiring time, it's quitting time." He grinned.

Mrs. Sanford had fire in her eye when we walked into the store together. "You're late!" she said to Jake.

"I'm done," he said.

"Done? Done with what?" she shouted. "You've

done nothing but shirk your chores since you set
yourself up with those two." She threw a quick
glance at us and then fastened her eyes on Jake again.
"I have told your father that you are no longer living
under my roof. What do you think of that, boy?"

Jake didn't stutter a bit as he stood right up to Mrs.
Sanford. "He's known that for weeks. My father
trusts me."

"More fool he!" she shouted. She was so angry that
spit flew out of her mouth as she talked. "You will
live under my roof or you will no longer work under
it."

"Good enough for me," said Jake. "Goodbye, Mrs.
Sanford." And we turned to go.

"Just a minute," she said. "Where—"

But we were already out the door.

Jake had held up well, but his eyes were big and he
looked scared to death as we stood outside the store.
Then Walter put his arm around him from one side
and I from the other and we half skipped, half
marched down the road to Simsbury.

Mr. Edmonds looked just as we'd left him weeks
ago. His hair still stuck out in all directions and he
was still poring over his account books. He did smile,
however, as we walked in. He leaned back in his
chair as we walked over to him.

"Remember us?" I said.

"You're unforgettable," he said, shaking his head

with a smile.

"This is Jake Whittingham," I said. "He's the third member of the team."

Jake smiled and nodded.

"Ah," said Mr. Edmonds, "the witness!"

He had a good memory; I'll give him that.

Jake bowed. "In person!" he said.

"Did you bring me some evidence on the river boys?"

"No," said Walter. "We brought you a deal."

"No evidence, no deal," Mr. Edmonds said, but he didn't turn back to his books. I think he liked us.

"Do you have a lockkeeper for the locks just north of here?" asked Walter.

"Not yet," he said. "Karl Meyer took a job in the mills. We're putting Tom Chapin in the lockhouse in Granby. He'll have his hands full fixing it up."

"There's been some damage at the Simsbury locks too," Walter said. "The locks are full of rocks, the shaft is missing on the intake and bent on the out-take, and the windows of the lockhouse have been broken."

"I know," said Mr. Edmonds. "I've been planning to get someone over there to do repairs."

"We're applying for the job," I said.

"Of lock repair?" he asked. His voice sounded like he thought this was all a joke.

"Lockkeeper," I said.

"All of you?"

"All of us."

"You're too young," he said.

"To do what?" I asked.

"To run the locks," he said.

"Let's see," I said. "To run the locks, you have to open and shut the gates at the right time, and you do that by pushing on the beams. The mules and the tow boys help you do that. You have to turn the handle on the shafts to let the water in or out, right? And the handle weighs what, about ten pounds? Which one of us do you think is too young to lift a ten-pound handle?"

"I don't know." He laughed, then he thought for a minute. "You could probably do those things, but there's more to it than that. Getting a boat through the locks is tricky. Everything's got to be timed perfectly or the boat will be swamped or stuck. Besides that, you've got to clean and inspect the locks, repair the damage to the lockhouse, keep the towpath clear of brush, and provide food and drink to the tow boys."

"Sounds like child's play to me," I said. "Isn't that fine? You've got the children to do it."

Mr. Edmonds laughed again and shook his head. The meeting seemed to be going pretty well.

"How much did you pay Karl Meyer for running the locks?" Walter asked.

"Twenty dollars a month plus free rent," he said.

"We'll do it for five dollars and the rent," I said.

"You can't handle it." His words were certain, but he didn't sound so sure any more.

"T-t-try us," said Jake. "Wha-wha-what have you got to leh-leh-lose?"

Mr. Edmonds glanced at us while Jake struggled to get the words out, but he didn't laugh. I was growing to like this man.

"You'll save fifteen dollars a month," I said.

"What about this evidence you were going to bring me?" Mr. Edmonds asked.

"Coming within the month," said Walter.

"You can't live in the lockhouse without an adult present," he said.

"My mother will be living with us," said Walter.

That was by no means certain, but I didn't glance at Walter. I kept my eyes on Mr. Edmonds.

"One month," he said. "During that time you'll repair any minor damage to the house, operate the locks once the canal opens, feed and put up the tow boys, and bring in evidence for the court of damage to the canal done by the river boys. Otherwise you're out." He wasn't laughing now.

Walter gulped. It was a tall order, but I didn't hesitate for a minute. I put out my hand. "Done and done," I said. Walter grinned and nodded.

16

Moving

Moving to the lockhouse meant saying goodbye to our little cabin in the woods. When the quilts were all folded and each of Walter's boxes together with Jake's things and mine were piled on the wagon we'd borrowed from the Wiltons, we took one more walk around the cabin. It had been the first home I'd had in a very long time.

When there was nothing left inside, Walter went out and climbed into the wagon. Jake and I followed. Walter slapped the reins and we started off. He kept his eyes straight ahead, but Jake and I were looking back.

There was, however, little time to spend much thought on what we'd left behind. It was nice to walk, bold as brass, into the lockhouse at Simsbury. We held our heads up high and carried our few belongings into our new home proudly even though nobody saw us.

While Walter took the horse and wagon back to the Wiltons, Jake and I set about cleaning up the lockhouse. Compared to the cabin, the lockhouse seemed enormous. It was three stories high with a staircase going right up the center of it. There was a room on either side on each floor.

We'd dismantled Walter's water gatherer from the cabin but neither of us could figure out how to put it together so we had to carry water up from the canal for the scrubbing.

When we'd chased away the dirt, Jake and I tried to make the lockhouse look like home as fast as we could. We put the broken furniture in the corner, hoping we could fix it later, and placed the few chairs and our table from the old place in the middle of the big room. We put Walter's boxes and barrels against one wall, although we knew he'd rearrange them when he got back. We set up the biggest bedroom on the second floor for Walter and Jake while I took the one closest to the locks. That left two bedrooms on the third floor for Walter's mother and Bertha. Emory could share a room with me. Other tow boys, when they came, would have to make do with bedrolls. Walter had said they'd mostly sleep outside, anyway.

There were even three beds there in pretty good shape, and we set them up along with the one we'd brought from the cabin. With Walter's mother's quilts on the beds, the bedrooms looked quite cheerful.

We worked fast and had things pretty settled by the time Walter was back. I was just putting up a branch of bittersweet for decoration on the longest wall when he walked in the door. He nodded when he saw what I was doing and, just as I thought, he rearranged all his boxes and barrels. Then he set about putting up the snowmelt (it would catch rainwater now instead of snow). He drilled a hole in the wall near the fireplace for the pipe. Jake and I cleaned out the fireplace, carrying the ashes to what would be our compost pile near the spot where our garden would go. Emory would have his garden.

Since the weather was warmer, we didn't need as many quilts on our beds, so I hung two of them—the log cabin on one wall of the big room and the yellow and white wedding ring on the other. Things began to look homey.

We still felt like visitors, but that night, when the lamp was lit, things looked better, even if it wasn't yet as cozy as the cabin. We ate our first supper around the table while admiring our handiwork. Then I sewed shoe tops while Jake and Walter worked at repairing some broken chairs.

Walter had gotten up before Jake and I the next morning and was scrubbing the floor.

"We did that yesterday," I said.

"I know," he said. "There were just a couple of spots you missed."

I shook my head and went back to the shoe tops.

When the floor seemed to meet with Walter's satisfaction, he and Jake went to haul wood. They took the wheelbarrow since there wasn't enough snow on the ground now to use the sled. I worked on shoe tops all day, keeping one eye on the canal.

Two men came up the towpath along about noon. I went out to meet them.

"You one of the children Edmonds was talking about?" asked one of the men, who was almost as short as me.

"Yessir, Etta Prentice," I said. "Are you with the canal?"

"Eh-yah," he said. "Walking the line. First boat's coming through soon. Gotta make sure it won't get stranded."

"May I know your names?" I asked. I hoped to establish a businesslike presence.

He looked surprised. You could tell he wasn't used to dealing with women in business. "This here's Zeke Hayes and I'm Tom Kibbe," said the short one.

"Pleasure to meet you, Mr. Hayes, Mr. Kibbe. How far up do you have to go?" I asked.

"To the Massachusetts line," Mr. Kibbe said. "Edmonds said there'd be a woman here. Where is she?" He looked around.

"Not here right now," I said. Well, that was true, wasn't it? "Is there something I can help you with?"

"Supposed to give her a list of the things you've got to get done here."

"List away," I said. "I'll get paper and pencil for you to write on."

"No need for that," he said. "Can't neither read or write."

We walked around the place together. They stopped when they got to the root cellar. "Got to get rid of this brush," said Mr. Hayes.

"Will do," I said. Apparently our disguise had worked; they didn't notice that there was a large hole beneath that brush. Still, it reminded me that we'd have to finish our root cellar very soon.

They set about replacing the shafts on the locks and then came to the door.

"You gotta get the rocks out of the lock," Tom Kibbe said, "put glass in these windows, clean this house up."

"It is clean," I said, quite offended. Oh my, was it clean. "This place is spotless."

"Sorry," they both said after looking quickly around the room.

I accepted their apology and they left.

The next day we started getting the rocks out of the lock, taking turns stepping into water that was just barely free of ice, tossing the stones out, then rushing into the house for dry clothes and to warm up by the fire. Then we went to town, where I paid for three panes of glass and some putty from my shoe top money. We fixed the windows as soon as we got back.

With Jake's help, Walter cleared out the brush and put steps and a frame on the root cellar. He fitted it with the door from the old, hidden root cellar. Then we piled our woodpile around it to hide it. We still hadn't quite figured out how we were going to use it, but we hoped the root cellar would be central to our plan when the time came.

The canal was about to open again. One packet boat was going to make the first run from Northampton to New Haven the next week.

That night, at supper, we were feeling pretty proud of ourselves.

"Well," I said, "we've done everything on the list for the canal folks. What's our next step?"

"The next step is for me to go to Granville and get Ma," Walter said. "We've got a nice place for her, and we've got to have an adult here or it's no go."

"I'm surprised you waited this long," I said. "I'd have thought you'd have her with you in the cabin."

"Wasn't a fit place to bring her," he said. "And she didn't want to come. Now she's got to."

"Maybe we'd all better go," I said. "She may need some persuading."

So the next morning we started up the mountain.

Golden saw us coming. He was at the end of the

drive when we got there and he was so delighted to see Walter, he got quite frisky. After giving the dog his attention, Walter led us all into the house.

Walter's mother met us at the door. This time her face was full of smiles. "Walter, dear," she said. "And Ella, was it?"

"It's Etta, Ma," said Walter. He kissed her cheek

"Of course. Please, sit down, Etta, and you too, Jake. Can I offer you a cup of tea?"

"I'll get it," said Walter, and he headed out to the kitchen. His mother sat down at the table and we joined her there.

To my surprise, the inside of the house was quite tidy. The table held the only clutter—scraps of cloth, scissors, and thread. The room didn't have much in it but it was neat. I could see where Walter got his living habits.

"I'm so glad that Walter's found such nice friends," said his mother. "For a while after he moved to Granby, he seemed very lonely."

"Wah-Wah-Walter's a g-g-good friend," said Jake.

"Do you live near each other?" she asked.

I thought that it was best left to Walter to explain our situation, so I picked up a strip of quilt top. Each piece was cut in a diamond shape and sewn together in one strip.

"Texas star?" I asked.

"Why, yes it is, dear. Do you quilt?"

"No, Mrs. Clark, I never have but I sure do admire your work." I wanted to tell her how wonderful it was to sleep under her warm quilts but there was time for that later.

Walter was back with the tea and, as we sipped it, he said, "Ma, I'd like you to come live in Simsbury with me."

"You're living in Simsbury?" she said. "I thought it was Granby."

"Simsbury," said Walter. "We're running the locks there. Got a nice house for you now."

"Oh, Walter, I don't think I can do it," she said, looking around at her things. "I've lived here since the day I was married, and now, with Roy's grave here . . ." She looked out the window toward the pasture, where we could see the pile of stones.

"We need your help," said Walter.

"My help?" She looked puzzled. "How on earth could I help? I'm old. I have no money."

"They won't let us stay there without an adult," Walter said. "And you're it."

"I'm it?" she asked.

"Eh-yah," Walter said. "And we need to capture a river boy." We all grinned at that. It did seem preposterous.

"What are you going to do with him once you've got him?" she asked.

"We're going to take him to the canal office," said

Walter determinedly. "But we've got to catch him in the act of doing damage to the canal."

"Do you know when the river boys will come?" His mother looked at each of us as she questioned her son.

"No," he said.

"Do you know *where* the river boys will come?"

"No," he said.

"Do you know how many there will be if they *do* come?"

"No."

"Do you know how you're going to capture one?"

"Sort of," I said.

She raised her eyebrows and looked at me.

"We've built a root cellar," Jake said.

Her eyebrows went up even higher.

"We're hoping a river boy will fall in," I said sheepishly. It did sound far-fetched.

Mrs. Clark smiled and shook her head. "Such a careful plan. I guess I could—for a short while, my dear," she said. "I'd like to see your new house, Walter, but I can't stay long."

"How will you get there, Ma?" Walter asked.

"I can get to Simsbury Center. Clyde Avery can bring me down in the wagon. He goes down every few days. Are you far from the town center, Walter?"

"No," said Walter. "Not far. We'll wait at the general store in Simsbury the day after tomorrow."

And he was out the door. Before we could follow, Walter was back. "Bring Golden," he said.

We murmured our goodbyes and left.

17

Houseguests

We met Mrs. Clark and Golden at Simsbury Center as planned. Walter and I stood on each side of his mother as we slowly walked to the house. Jake carried her bag. Golden kept putting his face between us as we went.

At the doorway of our lovely house we all watched for Mrs. Clark's reaction.

"Oh, my!" she said with a smile. "And this is your place, Walter?"

"Only if things go right, Ma," Walter said.

Mrs. Clark sat down in the big room. Golden spotted Minerva and immediately chased her up a tree. He was barking furiously while she snarled down at him.

"Why, this is lovely!" Walter's mother said, ignoring the ruckus outside. "You've made a lovely home for yourself, Walter."

"Ma, Etta and Jake live here too," he said. "We're in this thing together."

She looked first at Jake and then at me. "Well, it's

simply beautiful."

"Your quilts make it beautiful," I said.

"They do look pretty, don't they?" She smiled and patted my hand. She walked over to the wedding ring quilt and fingered it. "Sometimes I think making the quilts keeps me from losing my mind. Certainly their sales brought the only money in for a long time."

"I'll p-p-put your things upstairs," said Jake.

"Thank you, dear, but if it's all the same to you," said Mrs. Clark, "I'd be better off down here for the short time I'm here. Stairs are not easy for me these days." She seemed apologetic. "I'll just sleep here in this chair."

"No, we'll bring your bed down," said Walter as he started up the stairs. Jake went up to help.

"I hate to be such a bother," his mother called up after him.

"It's fine," I said. "It'll give us a chance to show off more of your quilts."

They set up her bed in the back corner of the room and covered it with a broken star quilt done in yellow and white. We put a small table with a lamp beside it and another sprig of bittersweet on the wall. As soon as it was set up, Mrs. Clark laid down and slept for several hours.

She got up for supper and, in the middle of the meal, there was a scraping noise at the door and Jake opened it to admit Golden. He looked around for

Minerva but she was nowhere in sight. Golden went to each of us to be petted and then lay down in front of the fire. Nobody said much that whole evening except to murmur to the dog. Jake went to the door every little while to call for Minerva, but she wouldn't come.

For the next few days we worried about Minerva, but most of our attention was on watching for the river boys at night and trying to come up with a plan for what would happen if and when they came.

The best we could do was to keep the door of the root cellar open at night, flat on the ground. We made a path between the woodpiles leading to and from the trap in a straight line from the lock, replacing the logs to hide the root cellar each morning and removing them each night. Vandals could step around the hole, of course, if they saw it in time, but we hoped that in the dark and in their hurry they wouldn't see it until it was too late. If we could somehow get the river boys to run in that direction, one of them might fall into the trap and we'd be able to close the door and sit on it. How we were going to get them to run across that very spot was uncertain. So was how we were going to keep the other boys from coming back to rescue a captive. We had to just keep careful watch and hope for the best.

During the daytime, we cleared brush, repaired the

outside of the house, and removed rocks from the towpath, the berm, and the locks. We put up a new outhouse and repaired the pump. Mrs. Clark sometimes stood in the doorway watching us. She thought everything we did was wonderful and she didn't hesitate to tell us so. It was nice, being appreciated like that. Plus, she took over the cooking and she was very good at it. I think even Walter was relieved.

One day Minerva came strolling back. Golden spotted her almost before we did and charged. This time Minerva didn't run up a tree but stood her ground, hissing with her back up. Golden growled and barked furiously but, as soon as he got close to Minerva, the cat swiped his nose with her claw. Golden yelped and ran to Walter for comfort. Minerva walked to the door and we let her in. In a little while, Golden came in too, but he steered a careful path around Minerva, who just watched from her table perch until Golden lay down.

Sometimes, after supper, we'd work on refining our plan, but we soon realized that it all depended on how many river boys came, where they'd be, what they were doing, and what they'd do when they saw us. We'd have to be on our toes, remember where the trap was, and try to head them toward it. One of us would have to be at the trap to close the door before they could scramble out. We all resolved to keep our wits about us and that was about all we could do.

Walter and I began to read aloud each night after supper. Most times Mrs. Clark would work on a quilt and listen but sometimes she'd take a turn. If it wasn't my turn to read, I'd work on shoe tops.

Later, we took turns keeping watch, usually two of us at a time, while the other slept. Near the end of the week, I was on watch one night with Jake.

"Mrs. Clark's a good cook," he said.

"She sure is," I said. "Walter was—"

Jake held up his hand. At first I thought it was to stop me from saying anything against Walter, but then I heard it too. There were soft voices coming from the canal. The water magnified the sound.

I ran up the stairs to get Walter. He must have been sleeping lightly for it took only one touch before he was on his feet and pulling on his clothes. We got back to Jake at the window.

"How many?" said Walter.

"Cah-cah-can't tah-tah-tell from here," Jake said. He crept toward the door, eased it open, and crawled out.

Walter was right behind him. I started to follow but Walter motioned me back.

As I watched with my eyes just above the sill, I could see Walter heading at an angle toward the woods to the right.

Walter motioned to me and, when I came out, he pointed up the middle. Staying close to the ground, we all converged on the sound of people talking.

As we got close, I still couldn't hear what they were saying but these were deep voices. If they were boys, they were pretty old boys. I stopped behind a tree and waited as I watched two men walk toward us on the towpath. Just before they got to us, they stopped and turned toward each other. In the moonlight, I could see that the one facing my direction was distinctly familiar. It was Mr. Wilton. He was speaking quietly to the other man. Apparently, these were just two men taking a stroll up the towpath. Still talking quietly, they turned and walked back in the direction they had come.

Softly we walked back into the house. "False alarm," I said.

"Who were they?" asked Jake.

"One was Mr. Wilton," I said. "I couldn't see the other man's face."

"It was Joe Hodge," Walter said. "His farm's down near Avon."

"What were they doing here in the middle of the night?" I asked.

"It's not the-the-the-that late," said Jake. "Just out for a walk, I guess. Shucks! I was hoping for a real fah-fah-fah-fight." He put up his fists and took up a fighting stance. He looked like a banty rooster.

"Tomorrow's another day," said Walter.

Jake and I resumed our watch positions and Walter went back to bed.

18

Walter's Story

Dear Etta,

It took some doing but I can come to Simsbury Friday evening, March 27th. It will cost me a day's pay but I won't have to be back at the boardinghouse until nine o'clock Sunday evening. I'll come on the mail coach and arrive in Simsbury some time before dark.

Looking forward to seeing your new home.

Your loving sister,

Bertha

The letter had come by post and I sat on the steps of the post office at Simsbury to read it. This was wonderful news and, as soon as I'd read it, I rushed home to tell the others and to write to Emory to arrange his visit for the same time.

"They're coming next Friday!" I announced as I ran in the door. Walter was just putting the noonday dinner on the table. He grinned. "Both of them?"

"Well, Bertha for sure," I said. "And I think Emory can get here then too. I'll write to him tonight."

"Your brother and sister, dear?" asked Walter's mother.

"Yes, Mrs. Clark," I said. "My family! You'll love them and they'll love you. They'll love this place too, when they see it and they'll want to—" I stopped. I had almost said too much.

Walter was looking out at the lock. "We've been here less than two weeks and we've put up shelves and insulated the root cellar, dug that huge pile of rocks out of the canal and the garden, and started a stone wall. There's still a lot to do but we've come a long way." His voice was proud.

I joined him at the window. He was right to be proud. We all were. Things were looking good. The lockhouse had been spruced up. The stones lining the lock above the water level had been scrubbed clean. The holes and ruts in the towpath were filled in. It no longer looked like an abandoned home.

When I went out later, Walter was clearing brush on the towpath. Jake was tending to the berm side of the canal. I picked up a hatchet and joined Walter.

After clearing a bit, I sat down and looked at Walter.

"Your mother is wonderful," I said.

He nodded and went on clearing brush.

"How could you have left her?"

"Pa."

"You left because your father drank?" There had to

be more to it than that.

"Pa drank and then he got mean," Walter said, not looking up from his work.

"He beat you?" I asked.

He nodded. "Whenever he thought of it," he said. "Maybe because he was just plain mean or maybe because he couldn't figure me out. He had no use for the canal. I came down here every chance I could just to be near it. He'd beat me every time he caught me. One night Pa just went wild. Beat me so hard with a stick that he knocked me out and then ran off."

"Were you hurt bad?" I asked.

He nodded. "Ma nursed me back."

"Then what happened?"

"I left." He looked hard at me as he said it.

I put down my hatchet and walked closer toward him. "You left and went to the foreman's cabin?"

"No," he said. "I left and hired out at the Wiltons."

"The Wiltons?" No wonder Wolf knew Walter so well; he'd lived with him.

"What about your mother?"

"She wouldn't come," he said.

"Why?"

"She said her place was there." Walter shook his head.

"Did your father beat her?"

"I dunno. I don't think so. I never saw him strike her except with words."

"How long did you stay at the Wiltons?"

"Couple of months."

"Didn't you like it there?"

"Liked it well enough."

"Why did you leave?"

"Pa found me. Threatened to burn down their barn and shoot Wolf. Had to go."

"To the cabin?"

"No, went to the Hodges."

"Then?"

"No," Walter smiled a bit. "No, I tried living all over the place. Hiring myself out wherever I could, but Pa kept finding me and I'd have to leave."

"Wha-wha-why did he do the-the-that?" Jake was back on our side. "Huh-huh-hunt you down, I mean?"

"I dunno." Walter shook his head. "Seemed like it was almost a game for him. Probably still be doing it if he hadn't died. Speaking of that, we've got to bury him right when this is over. We've got to bury him right."

He picked up his ax and walked over to the berm. The conversation was over.

19

The Visitors

I had picked three large bouquets of pussy willows and put one in the middle of the table in the front room and one in each bedroom on the third floor of the lockhouse.

With a lot of complaint and an equal amount of commotion, Walter and Jake had dismantled my bed and set it up again in Bertha's room. We'd made a pallet for Emory to sleep on in the other bedroom. We put the red and black log cabin quilt I'd slept under in the cabin on the bed and another on Emory's wall. The rooms looked quite cheerful.

After the others went downstairs, I stood in the hallway between the two bedrooms and imagined what fun it would be when the people I loved most were in them. What good times were coming! We had, for the first time, a real chance of being a family again.

Then I went to Simsbury Center to meet Bertha and Emory and bring them home at last.

The stage came in on time and Bertha stepped out.

She looked lovely with her pretty blue dress and bonnet—quite the fine lady. We hugged and waited, with our arms around each other, for Emory to arrive. Bertha chattered on about the work at the mill and the girls in the boardinghouse and a shopping trip they'd made to Springfield. I barely listened, keeping an eye on the road into town. In a matter of minutes Emory came running up the road from the other direction.

"Goodness, Emory," said Bertha. "Did you run all the way from Somers?"

"No," he said, laughing as he hugged us. "Mr. Evans brought me as far as Salmon Brook. I crossed the canal! Can we see the boats?"

"No boats yet," I said, "but one's due tomorrow. You may even get to see the first boat of the season come through our locks. Oh, wait till you see our house! You'll love it. It's perfect. Bertha, we've given you a room at the top where you can see down the canal for miles. And Emory, your room looks up the canal."

Bertha picked up her carpetbag and we walked down to the towpath and then headed north. Emory had a thousand questions about the canal and I tried to answer them without much success. There was so much I didn't know.

"Walter will be able to tell you everything," I said. "He knows all about the canal. Jake knows a lot about it too. Jake stammers sometimes and you can't make fun of him, all right? Just wait and he'll get the words out. Oh, you're going to love Jake and Walter, and his mother's there too."

There was no time to tell them more because we came within sight of the lockhouse. We stopped and they looked all around the clearing.

"Isn't it beautiful?" I asked.

Before they could say anything, Jake stepped out of the house. "Wah-wah-want to see how the lah-lah-lah-locks work?" he asked Emory.

"Sure!" Emory said, and they walked off together.

"That didn't take long," said Bertha. "Friends already." We walked into the house together.

Mrs. Clark was charming as ever and even Walter talked to Bertha a bit. So the evening turned out even better than I dared to hope. Walter's mother had prepared a fine supper and kept the conversation going. She talked to Emory about the farm and to Bertha about the mill. Both of them were obviously as taken by this gentle lady as I was.

We played my grandmother's trunk and charades after dinner, and the house was filled with laughter. In between turns, Walter was kept busy answering Emory's questions about the canal, although some explanations would have to wait for a demonstration.

"Why do you need locks?" Emory asked at one

point.

"To get from one level of the water to the next without going through waterfalls or rapids. Without them, where the land rises or falls, boats couldn't go up or down the canal at all. Wait for tomorrow, Emory," Walter said with a smile. "You'll see something then."

We all did. The next morning was a hectic one as we got everything ready for the first packet boat of the season to come down the canal. Many villagers had come over to watch. Mr. and Mrs. Wilton had come, and even Mrs. Sanford was there. Some people had brought picnic lunches to make a day of it, although it was windy and a bit raw. Still, everyone's spirits were high.

We heard the whistle toot three times to announce the boat's arrival. Everybody cheered as we saw the mule team come around the bend. They pulled a rope about two hundred feet long so far ahead of the boat that they seemed to have nothing to do with it, although, of course, the boat wouldn't be moving without them. Two boys walked along beside the mules and waved their hats as they came into sight. Emory was beside himself with excitement. He ran back and forth across the beams from berm to towpath. I was terrified he'd fall in but he was sure-footed. Fortunately Jake wasn't trying that. He was beside Bertha and me but we were all too excited to stand still. Mrs. Clark was beaming and chatting with some of the villagers.

Then we heard music. A group of musicians was sitting on the roof of the boat's cabin playing "Flow Gently, Sweet Afton." People laughed and cheered and we were all jumping up and down as they pulled up to the first gate. Emory ran over and began stroking the mules' necks and talking excitedly with the tow boys.

Getting the boat down from the higher level through the locks took some doing. Walter had closed the lower gate of the first lock and opened the higher one as soon as he had seen the mule team. The water began to rise in the lock. When it reached the right level, the mules led the boat forward until it nearly touched the closed gate. Now we needed to lower the boat. Emory, Bertha, and I pushed on the beam on one side while the mules led by the tow boys pushed on the other side to close the top gate. Jake and Walter turned the shaft to open the valve and the water level carrying the boat went down. When the water level in the lock was exactly the same as the level on the canal, the mules pulled on one side and we on the other and the lower gate opened.

The mules pulled the boat along to the next set of locks. Walter had closed the lower gate. The water released from the upper set of locks flowed in and the packet followed it into the lock. Jake was ready to turn the shaft that released the butterfly valve allowing the water out and the boat sank to the next level. So it went through the three locks in our charge. It took most of an hour before the boat came through the last lock. The tow boys fed and watered the mules before they came up to the house along with the captain of the boat, his first mate, and the three musicians.

"Good job, boys," said the captain, clapping Walter on the back.

"We'll do it faster next time," said Walter. "We were slow on that last gate."

We had a fine dinner of shepherd's pie waiting for them at the house and they ate hearty while Bertha and I fetched and served.

"Mighty fine vittles," said Captain Noble, wiping his mouth as he sat back in his chair.

"None finer," agreed the first mate.

Emory hung on every word the men spoke.

"What are you carrying?" Walter asked.

"Not much," said the captain. "Little lumber and some cider vinegar. This is really just a trip to check the workings. The real business won't get going for another week or so. We're checking to see that everything's the way it ought to be. Been a lot of damage this year. The locks in Southampton are so bad, we had a devil of a time getting through."

"River boys?" Walter asked.

"Maybe," said the captain. "Maybe so. Lots of folks have a lot of grudges against this thing."

The captain and crew got back on the boat; the musicians struck up a lively tune, and the tow boys got the mules moving forward. When they were a long way up the path, the boat began to move.

We stood on the towpath and waved them out of sight, then turned to each other.

"Weh-weh-we did it!" Jake cried and hugged me. Then everybody was hugging and dancing around. We had done it. We'd operated the locks, fed the crew, and we hadn't disgraced ourselves one little bit.

"The work's not over," Walter said. "With the canal opening, the river boys will be on the march. We've got to keep careful watch tonight."

"What will we do if they come?" Bertha asked.

"We've got kind of a plan," I said. "We're going to trap one in the root cellar."

Emory's eyes lit up. "Oh, I hope they come tonight. If they do, can I help?"

"If they come," I said, "we'll need all the help we can get."

Bertha looked wary. "What can we do?"

"How loudly can you yell?" Walter asked.

"Pretty loud. You have to talk really loud in the mills to be heard."

"Good! When I start yelling, you do the same."

"Doesn't seem like much of a plan," Bertha said.

"It'll do," Walter said.

20

Capture

Later, Walter and I sat in the darkened front room by the window, looking out at the canal and listening to the spring peepers, always the first sign of spring for me. Their rhythmic peep was so loud, it almost drowned out our conversation.

"Are they staying?" Walter asked.

"Who?" I asked.

"Bertha and Emory."

"Well, they're here. I don't know if they'll stay. I think Emory would like to, but Bertha doesn't want to leave the mill. How can she stand it, let alone like it?" I was talking as much to myself as to Walter. "It's noisy, dangerous work. How could she prefer to live in a boardinghouse when she could live here?"

"Everybody wants something different, I guess," he said.

"What do *you* want, Walter?" I turned toward him in the darkness.

"About what I've got," he said. "A chance to live out in the open. A place for my mother and me with room for a friend or two." He smiled at me. "And a job with the canal. If we can keep this place, that is."

It occurred to me then that with all my plotting, I'd never even asked Walter if it was all right to bring Bertha and Emory to live with us. "You knew all along I planned to ask them to live with us, didn't you, Walter," I said.

"Eh-yah," he said.

"Will it be all right with you if they come?" I asked, feeling guilty that I hadn't asked him before.

"Eh-yah," he said.

"Would you rather have—"

Walter held up his hand. He was looking out the window.

"What is it?" I whispered. "I didn't hear anything."

"Thought I saw something move," he said. He peered out through the window.

I looked out too. At first I couldn't see anything. Then part of the oak tree a few yards away seemed to separate from the trunk and move toward the canal. A person was crossing to the berm on the other side of the waterway.

"There is somebody out there," I whispered, turning to Walter, but he was gone. In the dim light I could see him at the top of the stairs, waking Jake, Bertha, and Emory. Mrs. Clark was up and standing beside me. Together we peered out into the darkness. When Golden growled, Mrs. Clark put her hand on his head. "Hush!" she said softly. The growling stopped.

We kept watch out the window and saw two other shadows depart the woods and stand on the gate top. "Still there?" Walter whispered. He was back with the others behind him.

His mother nodded and held up three fingers.

"Can't make our move too soon," he whispered. "Got to let them start the damage and then head them for the root cellar. Stay out of sight, but when the yelling starts, join in."

Walter eased the door open, and we followed him out. Jake motioned that he was heading to the root cellar. Walter, Emory, Bertha, and I crouched behind the towpath.

As my eyes got used to the darkness I could see three figures on top of the first gate. We crouched low and crept down beside the towpath until we were a good way beyond them. Walter whispered to Bertha to stay where she was until the shouting began. When we were well below the locks, Walter and I lowered ourselves into the water, trying not to gasp with the cold. Emory's look of dismay was clear but, with a shrug, he followed. As quietly as we could, we swam across the canal. The water was frigid. Clothing that had provided warmth now just soaked up the cold.

I wished I'd been quick enough to grab the job of

waiting at the root cellar before Jake had. I worried about how well Emory could swim but he seemed to be doing all right. In seconds I'd lost all feeling in my legs. Once on the berm side, we pulled ourselves out of the water as quietly as we could and headed into the woods in order to come up behind them. The chill air on my wet skin made my teeth chatter and I held my hand over my mouth. I used the other arm to hug Emory, but he was as chilled through as I was and cold comfort.

The root cellar was in a direct line from where the river boys were working to wedge logs into the gate. They worked almost soundlessly and we tried to be just as quiet as we took positions about ten feet behind them.

Then Walter hollered, "Get 'em!" and I yelled, "There they are!" Emory waved his arms and yelled, "After them, men!" We ran toward them, hollering and waving our arms. From up on the other side of the lock we could hear Bertha yelling, "Stop! Thief!" The river boys headed in the direction of the lockhouse.

Mrs. Clark yelled, "Sic 'em, Golden!" and the dog burst out barking to give chase. The river boys veered away from the house. Golden ran faster while Mrs. Clark yelled, "There goes one!"

We could see them running over the towpath. Two of them ran off into the woods but, wonder of all wonders, one took the path through the woodpile with Golden right behind him. Ignoring the escapees, we all ran toward the woodpile, making as much commotion as we could. There was a yelp, a crash and a thud in quick order, then Jake yelled, "I gah-gah-gah-got him! I gah-gah-gah-got him! Oh cah-cah-cah-come! I gah-gah-gah-got him!"

Golden stood wagging his tail with excitement on the cellar door. Jake was jumping up and down on it so hard I was afraid he'd crash through it. I put my hand on his shoulder to calm him down and patted and thanked Golden. Everybody thanked the dog. We all stood around the edges of the door, catching our breath, now completely unaware of the cold. Walter's mother came out with the lantern. As she approached, I looked around me at the grinning faces.

"Are you sure he's in there?" Walter asked Jake. Not a sound came from the other side of the door. "How do you know you got him?"

"I–I–I–," Jake was too excited to get the words out. He was laughing and trying to speak at the same time.

We were all laughing and slapping each other on the back.

"Shall we look?" I asked.

"Oh, let's!" Bertha said. "I want to see what a river boy looks like."

"No," Walter said. "No use taking a chance on letting him escape in the dark."

"Wha-wha-what if he's huh-hurt?" Jake asked.

"Doubt if he's hurt too much," Walter said. "It's not that deep and the floor is dirt. We've all fallen farther than that lots of times."

"He could have br-broken something," Jake said.

"Unless it's his neck, he'll live till morning," Walter said.

"Wha-what if he freezes to de-de-death?"

"He won't freeze," I said. "He's warmer than we are down there." Now that the excitement was over, I realized how very cold I was.

"You're right," Mrs. Clark said. "We should get you all into warm clothes or you'll be the ones freezing to death."

Walter's grin was gleeful. He piled some logs on top of the door. "Stay on top of him while we change, Jake. I'm going to sit here on this door until morning."

"We all will," I said.

"Then in the morning will we open the door?" asked Jake.

"No," I said. "Then we get Mr. Edmonds."

After we had changed into warm dry clothes, we did sit on that door all night. No one wanted to go to bed, although of course we could have taken turns. Jake brought out some nuts and apples. Mrs. Clark appeared with hot sweet cider. Golden and Minerva lay down among us and gave out some warmth. The woodpiles cut off some of the cold, and with lots of quilts and the lantern, it was really quite pleasant. We kept hugging each other, talking about how it had gone, slapping each other on the back, and laughing. Mrs. Clark congratulated us all and went to bed.

Then, when we'd gotten warm and settled down a bit, Emory began to sing. *"Flow gently sweet Afton among thy green braes."* His voice was high and beautiful. There were so many new things to discover about my family. And, if things went right, we'd have plenty of time.

We let Emory go through the first verse alone. Then we all chimed in. *"Thou stock dove whose echo resounds from the hill."* The tune was mournful and the words even more so, but we grinned through it all, so proud of ourselves, and went on to sing others, "Rock of Ages," "Lead Kindly Light." Bertha took up a descant and Walter tried for the bass. We went on to popular songs like "Long, Long Ago" and "Kathleen Mavourneen." Our root cellar guest got a lovely concert, although I'm not sure he was in any mood to appreciate our harmony.

We all slept a bit as the night went on but we kept waking up to congratulate each other again.

In the morning, Jake ran to the canal office to get the constable and Mr. Edmonds. We took turns going in for breakfast but we ate it back at the root cellar. Although our prisoner had made no attempt to get out, we didn't want to take any chances.

We were all back sitting on the door when we heard Jake's holler and looked up to see him pulling Mr. Edmonds by the hand. Coming close behind him was the town constable. Mrs. Clark came out to join us so it was quite a group to greet them.

"Well," Mr. Edmonds said, struggling to catch his breath. "What have we here?"

"What we have there, sir," I said, pointing to the log sticking out of the first gate, "is damage done by the river boys, and what we have here, sir," I tapped on the root cellar door with my foot, "is one trapped river boy."

We removed the logs from the door and stepped back. Mr. Edmonds and the constable walked over to the gate and surveyed the damage. We stayed close to the door though, ready to grab the prisoner should he try to escape.

They came back from the locks. "No doubt that damage has been attempted," said the constable.

Mr. Edmonds opened the root cellar door slowly. We all peered insde. There, blinking up at us in the sudden light, was a very miserable Mr. Wilton.

21

Success, Sort of

My first thought was that there had been some terrible mistake. Here we thought we had trapped a vandal but instead somehow, we had captured a respectable farmer. We owed him an apology. I was trying to figure out what went wrong as he came slowly up the root cellar stairs.

"Mr. Wilton?" Walter was the first to speak. "What?"

"Wilton!" Mr. Edmonds didn't seem the least bit apologetic. "What in the name of all that's holy did you think you were doing?"

"Trying to stop the canal," Mr. Wilton said. Now he looked squarely into Mr. Edmonds' eyes. "Put it out of business. There's a whole bunch of us, working up and down this thing to do as much damage as we can. It's got to be stopped."

"Farmers?" I said. "It's farmers, not river boys?" I couldn't believe it.

"Mostly farmers," Mr. Wilton said. "Occasionally river boys."

"Why?" I asked. "Why would you want to damage this beautiful canal?"

The constable spoke before Mr. Wilton could answer. "Jake said there were others with you, Wilton," said the constable. "Who were they?"

"Farmers like me. Folks that want to stop the canal."

"I need their names, Wilton." The constable looked grim.

"You won't get them from me," Mr. Wilton said. He turned to me. "The canal took our land without a by-your-leave. They split my farm to dig it. Then they cut costs and didn't build the embankments right. The damned thing leaks. It's turned my south pasture into a swamp. The sooner we can get the corporation to declare bankruptcy and fill the thing in with dirt, the better off we'll be."

He turned to Walter. "I'm sorry, Walter," he said. "I know you love the canal and I might too if it hadn't done so much damage. My farm supports my family."

The constable took Mr. Wilton by the arm and led him off.

"Will he have to go to jail?" Emory asked.

"Doubt it," said Mr. Edmonds. "He'll have to go to court, but they'll probably just fine him." He watched the men until they were out of sight.

"He's right about a lot of things," he said. "This

canal can be good for the farmers, but the corporation made a lot of mistakes. I don't know. They say
the railroad's coming and that will do us in before the
vandals can." He was looking down at his feet and
seemed to be talking as much to himself as he was to
us. Then he took a deep breath and looked up.
"However, you did what you said you'd do and so
the deal is made. You'll get the lockhouse to live in
and five dollars a month as long as a responsible
adult lives with you." He nodded toward Mrs. Clark
but she didn't appear to notice.

The others began to cheer and jump up and down
so Walter and I may have been the only ones to hear
him add, "You'll also get a food allowance to feed
the tow boys and their mules or horses."

That set us all off again, and it was some time
before we calmed down enough to realize that Mr.
Edmonds had gone. We headed back into our house.

Then, too soon, it was over. Bertha had to hurry to
catch the afternoon stage back to Stafford Springs,
and Emory decided to leave then too.

We walked together into Simsbury Center.

"Well, we've got a home at last," I said. "Isn't it
wonderful?"

"It is wonderful," said Bertha. "You've got the
perfect place for yourself, Etta. I love Jake and Walter
and his mother. It's all very nice and I've had a
lovely time."

"Right! The canal is great!" Emory said. "It was really fun capturing the bad man. Can I come back sometime?"

"Oh, Emory," I said, "of course you can come back. This is for us. I've done all this for us. As you've seen, there's plenty of room for you and Bertha to come and live there. Bertha can leave the mill and you can leave the farm. There's more than enough work with the canal for us all. We'll be a family again, don't you see?"

Emory looked thoughtful but said nothing. He hugged and kissed me and then hurried off toward Mr. Evans and the wagon that waited for him. "See you soon, Etta," he said.

Bertha walked for a while with her eyes straight ahead. Then she turned to me. "It is lovely at the lockhouse, Etta," she said, "but I'm not sure it's the life for me. It's so far away from everything."

"You can't mean that you prefer that awful mill and the boardinghouse to the lockhouse, Bertha," I said.

The stage was there, loaded and waiting. "Listen," she said. "Working in the mill is hard, but the money is good and we have good times, really, Etta, we do. And we get to Springfield often. I've got to go," she said. "I'll write." She hugged me and climbed aboard. I followed her and spoke through the open door as she crowded in with the other passengers.

"Bertha," I said, "we could be a family again. How can you even think of letting that go?" I tried to hold back the tears but they came full force. She had her face buried in her handkerchief and couldn't speak. Then the door closed and the stage drove off.

22

Family

The next few days went quickly and without much excitement. A few boats came though without incident. Jake and Walter happily assisted with their passage through the locks and I helped Mrs. Clark with the meals, but my thoughts were still on my family.

One afternoon Walter and I were sitting on the steps; he was mending a chair while I sewed shoe tops.

"Are they coming to stay?" he asked.

"Bertha will come eventually, I think," I said. "But Emory will come, I'm sure."

"Eh-yah, if you make him," he said.

"For this to be my home," I said firmly, "my family has to be here. You've got your family, Walter. Now I need mine."

"And Jake?" he asked.

"Jake's different," I said. "His mother and father would take him back in a minute if he'd live with the Shakers. He's got that choice."

"Emory and Bertha have choices too," he said.

"This is the best choice," I said firmly.

Monday morning I left the others and took the mail coach to Somers. A man in the general store there directed me to the Evans farm on the Enfield road, about four miles outside of town. The road led through woods for quite a way and I could hear robins and an ovenbird. The songbirds were back, although there was still quite a chill in the air and I was glad of my shawl.

I came upon a large cleared area bounded by white board fencing. Several small red outbuildings stretched out from a good-sized barn. There were a dozen or so guernsey cows milling about in the muddy barnyard next to the silo. Several watched me intently as I walked by. The white farmhouse stood against a small hill. A large maple tree in the door-yard bore a rope swing. Funny, Emory had said the Evanses had no children.

Emory said he loved the farm and I knew lots of folks did love farming. I'd never liked it much. Lots of hard work and raising animals in order to kill them seemed kind of heartless to me. Still, I ate the food they raised. Glad I didn't have to do the killing, though. Even chickens, noisy messy critters that they were. I didn't like to kill them, though I had often enough.

The only answer to my knock at the farmhouse

door came in the form of a large black dog that I thought for a minute was Wolf. He came dashing around the house barking wildly. I looked around for help but there was none. Fortunately, the dog stopped about six feet from me, but he continued his frenzied barking. He wasn't about to let me move very far.

"Thunder! Hush!" a man shouted and the dog's barking ceased immediately. Mr. Evans came around the corner of the house. He patted the dog, who rushed over to him. He smiled. "You're Emory's sister," he said. "Come to see him?"

"Yessir," I said.

"He's up with the lambs," he said. "Come on."

Thunder walked on one side of him and I on the other. As I've said, I'm not afraid of dogs, but there's no reason to tempt fate. "Emory says you're wanting him to live with you," Mr. Evans said.

"He's my family," I said. "I've got a good home for him now."

"I know," he said. We walked on together. Then he said, "We think a lot of Emory."

"So do I." I wasn't giving an inch.

"I can't blame you for wanting him with you," Mr. Evans said. "If he was my brother, I'd want the same, but you need to know this. Emory's a born farmer. He's good with the animals and he's good with the soil. He loves farming, and I doubt he'll be happy doing much else."

"I've got a place for him to garden," I said. "We've got animals too." I didn't mention that the animals consisted of a dog and a cat.

"It isn't a farm though, is it?"

Our conversation got no further, because at that moment Emory came around the corner of the barn. Thunder rushed over to him and jumped up and licked his face. Emory patted him and then looked over at us. "Etta!" he yelled and ran toward me with his arms outstretched.

When we'd finished hugging, I looked around for Mr. Evans but he was gone. "Come see the lambs," Emory said.

He led me to a small pasture where a half dozen ewes stood with their lambs close by. Several were nursing. Emory climbed over the fence and knelt down in the dirt beside the closest lamb. He put his arms around its legs and carefully picked it up. He brought it to the fence. The ewe walked with him, nuzzling first him and then her lamb. "Isn't he beautiful, Etta?" he said. "Feel his wool."

I nervously patted the lamb, but the ewe wasn't happy with my attentions. She was heading toward me with a mean look in her eye. I looked around. Each ewe eyed me warily.

"I thought you said there were seven lambs," I said, stepping back from the fence.

Emory put the lamb back in the field where its mother checked it over carefully. "Yes," he said. "We lost one. The mother's still grieving. She's in the barn."

We walked back toward the farmhouse. Emory sat in the swing and began to go slowly back and forth, feet still on the ground.

"You love it here, don't you?" I asked, but I knew the answer.

"I really do," he said. "But Etta, I've been thinking. I can come live with you at the lockhouse."

"I know you can," I said, "and I really want you to but I think . . ." This was hard to say. I took a deep breath. "I think maybe you ought not to."

"Really, Etta?" he said. He stopped swinging. "You really think it's all right for me to stay here?"

"I really do," I said.

"What about you though, Etta?"

"Em, I've worked so hard to get us all together. I never thought much about what you and Bertha wanted. I wanted it back the way it was, but it can't be the way it was with Ma and Pa no matter what I do. They died. And that changed everything. And Bertha likes the mill, goodness knows why, and you belong here. You know it, Mr. Evans knows it, and now I know it too. I've got a place for us now but there's no 'us' to put there."

He stood and hugged me. "There will always be an

us. Families don't have to live under the same roof to be families, do they?"

"Of course not." I was smiling, but tears were rushing down my face.

"We're still family, right?" he said.

I couldn't speak so I just nodded.

Mr. Evans came out of the farmhouse with a young woman. She was short and kind of round. She smiled at me but her eyes went directly to Emory as they walked toward him.

"Emory?" she asked.

"Staying," he said. He was wiping his cheeks fiercely. So was I.

Immediately her eyes filled with tears and she hugged him, "Oh, Emory," she said. "I'm so glad."

Mr. Evans put his arm around Emory's shoulders and looked at me. "Tough decision," he said.

"None tougher," I said.

Emory walked back to the center of Somers with me. "Mr. Evans says I can come to Simsbury any time I want to and stay as long as I want," he said.

"They're good people, I guess," I said.

"None better," he said.

23

Settling In

Supper was on and the others were at the table when I came in the door.

Walter looked up. "All right?" he asked.

"Guess so," I said.

He said nothing more but looked carefully at me. I slowly shook my head. He nodded and I thought he understood.

I picked at my supper but the others ate heartily. Mrs. Clark must have done the cooking. When the meal was over, she said, "Walter, it's time for me to go home."

Jake and I had been clearing the dishes but we stopped still. We looked at Walter.

"Ma," he said.

"I can't just abandon the place in Granville. It's my home," she said.

I probably should have let Walter and his mother work that out themselves, but I'd already lost too much that day. I wasn't sure whether this was a home we had here or just a household, but it was working.

We were working and having fun together—most of the time. I liked Jake and Walter, and Walter's mother, well, she was just the best. This wasn't family, but it was something very close.

"Mrs. Clark," I said. "Please stay. Families belong together."

"And you've all made yourselves into a very nice family." She smiled and patted my hand. She walked over to hug Walter. He kept his head down. "Walter's always been my family, but he's been on his own a long time and he's done very well for himself." Her voice was proud. Her outstretched hand swept the room. "Just look at all he's accomplished. And he has you and Jake. Walter can handle this and lots more. He doesn't need me."

"We do, though," I said. "Walter gets kinda cranky when you're not around."

"I'm not cranky," Walter said. "Just particular."

"Fuh-fuh-fussy," Jake said, laughing.

"He always did like things neat. Walter, I can't stay," she said. "There's the house in Granville."

"Sell it," Walter said. "Clyde Avery's been wanting it for pasture and a wood lot. The house isn't worth anything. Sell the land."

Mrs. Clark smiled tentatively.

"Your father . . ." she began.

"Should be buried," Walter said. He looked up at last. "We've got money enough now to do it right.

We'll go to Granville, hire the undertaker, and buy a grave in the cemetery and bury him right."

"It's a little like going through the locks, Mrs. Clark," I said. "The boat can't go forward until the level ahead is exactly right. We've got the lock-house—that's the level behind us now. But there're things up ahead. If you go back to Granville, Mrs. Clark, we might not be able to get to the next level."

Jake added, "If you leave, we-we-we'd huh-huh-have to eat Walter's cooking."

Walter shot Jake a look and then grinned at his mother. "I think all the votes are in," he said. "Best you stay."

Mrs. Clark walked over to the window and stared out. Nobody said a word. Nobody moved. She was smiling when she turned back to us. "Best I do," she said.

Afterword

Although this is a work of fiction, it is based on fact. There was a real Etta Prentice—my grandmother—and I've used some of the details of her life, although I've put her back a generation in order to involve the canal and its workings. The character of Walter is loosely based on my grandfather, who was on his own from the age of ten.

The Farmington Canal was started in 1825 with the intent of allowing the port of New Haven to serve as a depot for goods going to and coming from the farms and towns west of the Connecticut River. In 1829 it was open from New Haven to Farmington and, in 1835, it was open all the way to Northampton, Massachusetts, where it entered the Connecticut River. The first company went bankrupt and it was later reformed as the New Haven and Northampton Canal Company.

Problems beset the canal from the beginning. The soil in many places was not good for holding water and the canal often ran dry. It cost much more to build than the planners had expected and so they cut costs while constructing it. The banks washed out during big storms and, of course, ice blocked it in the winter.

Many of the farmers—like Mr. Wilton in this story—were very unhappy about the taking of their land to build the canal. Some farmers filed lawsuits and others did damage to the canal. However, it was the railroads that finally ended the canals in New England. Railroads were faster, less affected by the weather, and, in the end, cheaper to run. Shortly after the time of this book, the railroad purchased the canal property, perhaps opening up a new career for Walter and Etta.

Glossary

Berm – A raised bank especially along a canal. Usually the berm was on one side of the canal and the towpath on the other.

Broadfall – A style of trousers.

Double Rip – Two sleds tied together in a line.

Eh-yah – This is a slang variation of the word "yes." It was very common in New England at the time and can still be heard there, especially in Maine. Sometimes, it is pronounced "eh-yup."

Privy – An outhouse.

Quilts – There are several quilt patterns mentioned in this book: Log cabin, eight hands round, bow tie, wedding ring, and other designs. All involve the careful sewing together of pieces of material in a repeated pattern.

Waumas – A type of outerwear that is a cross between a sweater and a coat.